D0778242

"We need to go [...] *if we stay out h*[...] *moment longer, I'll be forced to kiss you."*

And there it was, out in the open. This thing...

"And you don't want to?" It was a whisper, so low Matt thought he'd misheard. But he hadn't. Penny's whisper seemed to echo. Even the owls above their heads seemed to pause to listen.

Did he want to?

This was such a bad idea. This woman was his employee. She was trapped here for the next four days, or longer if she took him up on his offer to extend.

What was he doing? Standing in the dark talking of kissing a woman?

Did he want to?

"Yes," he said, because there was nothing else to say.

"Then what's stopping you?"

"Penny..."

"Just shut up, Matt Fraser, and kiss me."

And what was a man to say to that?

Matt took Penny into his arms and he kissed her.

Dear Reader,

The first time I visited my husband's family farm was shearing time. I was warmly welcomed by my soon-to-be mother-in-law, who was overjoyed to have another pair of hands. Grace was up to her ears in baking.

The faster shearers work, the quicker they're paid, and at the pace they work, their demand for food is mind-blowing. What's more, the quality of their "tucker" often means not getting the gun-shearing teams or—horror—being relegated to winter shearing time. But Dave's farm had no such difficulty. On her ancient woodstove, Grace produced an extraordinary array of pies, cakes, slices, tarts, casseroles...you name it. Her sponge cakes alone would have induced any shearing team to stay.

So this is a book to celebrate the legend of Grace. Grace would be proud of my heroine, as Penny wins over her team of shearers—plus, of course, her very own boss-cum-billionaire. Grace would approve.

Enjoy.

Marion

Stranded with the Secret Billionaire

Marion Lennox

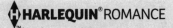

If you purchased this book without a cover you should be aware
that this book is stolen property. It was reported as "unsold and
destroyed" to the publisher, and neither the author nor the
publisher has received any payment for this "stripped book."

APR - - 2017

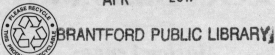

BRANTFORD PUBLIC LIBRARY

Recycling programs
for this product may
not exist in your area.

This work includes words based
on "THE SERENITY PRAYER"
by Reinhold Niebuhr.

ISBN-13: 978-0-373-74428-2

Stranded with the Secret Billionaire

First North American Publication 2017

Copyright © 2017 by Marion Lennox

All rights reserved. Except for use in any review, the reproduction or
utilization of this work in whole or in part in any form by any electronic,
mechanical or other means, now known or hereinafter invented, including
xerography, photocopying and recording, or in any information storage
or retrieval system, is forbidden without the written permission of the
publisher, Harlequin Enterprises Limited, 225 Duncan Mill Road,
Don Mills, Ontario M3B 3K9, Canada.

This is a work of fiction. Names, characters, places and incidents are
either the product of the author's imagination or are used fictitiously,
and any resemblance to actual persons, living or dead, business
establishments, events or locales is entirely coincidental.

This edition published by arrangement with Harlequin Books S.A.

For questions and comments about the quality of this book,
please contact us at CustomerService@Harlequin.com.

® and ™ are trademarks of Harlequin Enterprises Limited or its
corporate affiliates. Trademarks indicated with ® are registered in the
United States Patent and Trademark Office, the Canadian Intellectual
Property Office and in other countries.

HARLEQUIN®

Printed in U.S.A.

™ www.Harlequin.com

Marion Lennox has written more than a hundred romances and is published in over a hundred countries and thirty languages. Her multiple awards include the prestigious RITA® Award (twice) and the *RT Book Reviews* Career Achievement Award for "a body of work which makes us laugh and teaches us about love."

Marion adores her family, her kayak, her dog and lying on the beach with a book someone else has written. Heaven!

Books by Marion Lennox

Harlequin Romance

The Logan Twins

Nine Months to Change His Life

The Larkville Legacy

Taming the Brooding Cattleman

Sparks Fly with the Billionaire
Christmas at the Castle
Christmas Where They Belong
The Earl's Convenient Wife
His Cinderella Heiress
Stepping into the Prince's World

Visit the Author Profile page
at Harlequin.com for more titles.

This book is dedicated to the memory of Grace, the warmest, most generous mother-in-law a woman could wish for—and the baker of the world's best ginger fluff sponge!

CHAPTER ONE

THE IMPECCABLE ENGLISH ACCENT had directed Penelope Hindmarsh-Firth twelve hundred kilometres across two states without a problem. From 'Take the third exit after the Harbour Tunnel', as Penny had navigated her way out of Sydney, to 'Continue for two hundred kilometres until you reach the next turn', as she'd crossed South Australia's vast inland farming country, the cultured voice hadn't faltered.

True, the last turn had made Penny uneasy. The accent had told her to proceed for thirty kilometres along the Innawarra Track, but it had hesitated over the pronunciation of Innawarra. Penny had hesitated too. The country around them was beautiful, lush and green from recent rains and dotted with vast stands of river red gums. The road she'd been on had been narrow, but solid and well used.

In contrast, the Innawarra Track looked hardly used. It was rough and deeply rutted.

Penny's car wasn't built for rough. She was driving her gorgeous little sports car. Pink. The car had been her father's engagement gift to her, a joyful signal to the world that Penny had done something he approved of.

That hadn't lasted. Of course not—when had

pleasing her father lasted? Right now she seemed to be doing a whole lot wrong.

She was facing a creek crossing. It had been raining hard up north. She'd heard reports of it on the radio but hadn't taken much notice. Now, what looked to be a usually dry creek bed was running. She got out of the car, took off her pink sandals and walked across, testing the depth.

Samson was doing no testing. Her little white poodle stood in the back seat and whined, and Penny felt a bit like whining too.

'It's okay,' she told Samson. 'Look, it only comes up to my ankles, and the nice lady on the satnav says this is the quickest way to Malley's Corner.'

Samson still whined, but Penny climbed back behind the wheel and steered her little car determinedly through the water. There were stones underneath. It felt solid and the water barely reached the centre of her tyres. So far so good.

Her qualms were growing by the minute.

She'd estimated it'd take her two hours tops to reach Malley's, but it was already four in the afternoon and the road ahead looked like an obstacle course.

'If worst comes to worst we can sleep in the car,' she told Samson. 'And we're getting used to worst, right?'

Samson whined again but Penny didn't. The time for whining was over.

'Malley's Corner, here I come,' she muttered. 'Floods or not, I'm never turning back.'

Matt Fraser was a man in control. He didn't depend on luck. Early in life, luck had played him a sour hand and he hadn't trusted in it since.

When he was twelve, Matt's mother had taken a job as a farmer's housekeeper. For Matt, who'd spent his young life tugged from one emotional disaster to another, the farm had seemed heaven and farming had been his life ever since. With only one—admittedly major—hiccup to impede his progress he'd done spectacularly well, but here was another hiccup and it was a big one. He was staring out from his veranda at his massive shearing shed. It was set up for a five a.m. start. His team of crack shearers was ready but his planning had let him down.

He needed to break the news soon, and it wouldn't be pretty.

Hiring gun shearers was half the trick to success in this business. Over the years Matt had worked hard to make sure he had everything in place to attract the best, and he'd succeeded.

But this afternoon's phone call had floored him.

'Sorry, Matt, can't do. The water's already cut the Innawarra Track to your north and they're saying the floodwaters will cut you off from the south by tomorrow. You want to hire me a helicopter? It's the only alternative.'

A helicopter would cut into his profits from the wool clip but that wouldn't bother him. It was keeping his shearers happy that was the problem. No matter whose fault it was, an unhappy shed meant he'd slip down the shearers' roster next year. He'd be stuck with a winter shear rather than the spring shears that kept his flocks in such great shape.

So he needed a chopper, but there were none for hire. The flooding up north had all available helicopters either hauling idiots out of floodwater or, more mundanely, dropping feed to stranded stock.

He should go and tell them now, he thought.

He'd cop a riot.

He had to tell them some time.

Dinner was easy. They had to provide their own. It was only at first smoko tomorrow that the proverbial would hit the fan.

'They might as well sleep in ignorance,' he muttered and headed out the back of the sheds to find his horse. Nugget didn't care about shearing and shearing shed politics. His two kelpies, Reg and Bluey, flew out from under the house the moment they heard the clink of his riding gear. They didn't care either.

And, for the moment, neither did Matt.

'Courage to change the things that can be changed, strength to accept those things that can't be changed and the wisdom to know the difference...' It was a good mantra. He couldn't hire a chopper. Shearing would be a surly, ill-tempered disaster but it was tomorrow's worry.

For now he led Nugget out of the home paddock and whistled the dogs to follow.

He might be in trouble but for now he had every intention of forgetting about it.

She was in so much trouble.

'You'd think if there were stones at the bottom of one creek there'd be stones at the bottom of every creek.' She was standing on the far side of the second creek crossing. Samson was still in the car.

Her car was in the middle of the creek.

It wasn't deep. She'd checked. Once more she'd climbed out of the car and waded through, and it was no deeper than the last.

What she hadn't figured was that the bottom of this section of the creek was soft, loose sand. Sand that sucked a girl's tyres down.

Was it her imagination or was the water rising?

She'd checked the important things a girl should know before coming out here—like telephone reception. It was lousy so she'd spent serious money fitting herself out with a satellite phone, but who could she ring? Her father? *Dad, come and get me out of a river.* He'd swear at her, tell her she was useless and tell his assistant to organize a chopper to bring her home.

That assistant would probably be Brett.

She'd rather burn in hell.

So who? Her friends?

They'd think it was a blast, a joke to be bruited all over the Internet. Penelope Hindmarsh-Firth, indulged daughter of a billionaire, stuck in the outback in her new pink car. A broken engagement. A scandal. Her first ever decision to revolt.

There wasn't one she would trust not to sell the story to the media.

Her new employer?

She'd tried to sound competent in her phone interview. Maybe it would come to that, but he'd need to come by truck and no truck could reach her by dark.

Aargh.

Samson was watching from the car, whimpering as the water definitely rose.

'Okay,' she said wearily. 'I didn't much like this car anyway. We have lots of supplies. I have half a kitchen worth of cooking gear and specialist ingredients in those boxes. Let's get everything unloaded, including you. If no one comes before the car goes under I guess we're camping here while my father's engagement gift floats down the river.'

There was a car in the middle of the creek.

A pink car. A tiny sports car. Cute.

Wet. Getting closer to being swept away by the minute.

Of all the dumb...

There was a woman heaving boxes from some sort of luggage rack she'd rigged onto the back. She was hauling them to safety.

A little dog was watching from the riverbank, yapping with anxiety.

Matt reined to a halt and stared incredulously. Reg and Bluey stopped too, quivering with shock, and then hurled themselves down towards what Matt thought must surely be a hallucination. A poodle? They'd never seen such a thing.

The woman in the water turned and saw the two dogs, then ran, trying to launch herself between the killer dogs and her pooch.

She was little and blonde, and her curls twisted to her shoulders. She was wearing a short denim skirt, a bright pink blouse and oversized pink earrings. She was nicely curved—very nicely curved.

Her sunglasses were propped on her head. She looked as if she was dressed for sipping Chardonnay at some beachside café.

She reached the bank, slipped in the soft sand and her crate fell out of her hands.

A teapot fell out and rolled into the water.

'Samson!' She hauled herself to her feet, yelling to her poodle, but Reg and Bluey had reached their target.

Matt was too stunned to call them off, but there was no need. His dogs weren't vicious. This small mutt must look like a lone sheep, needing to be returned to the flock. Rounding up stray sheep was what his dogs did best.

But Matt could almost see what they were thinking as they reached the white bit of fluff, skidded to a halt and started the universal sniffing of both ends. *It looks like a sheep but...what...?*

He grinned. The troubles of the day took a back seat for the moment and he nudged Nugget forward.

There wasn't a thing he could do about his shearing problems. What he needed was distraction, and this looked just what the doctor ordered.

She needed a knight on a white charger. This was no white charger, though. The horse was huge and black as night. And the guy on it?

Instead of armour, he wore the almost universal uniform of the farmer. Moleskin pants. A khaki shirt, open at the throat, sleeves rolled to the elbows. A wide Akubra hat. As he edged his horse carefully down the embankment she had the impression of a weathered face, lean, dark, strong. Not so old. In his thirties?

His mouth was curving into a smile. He was laughing? At her?

'In a spot of bother, ma'am?'

What she would have given to be able to say: *No bother—everything's under control, thank you.*

But her car was sinking and Samson was some-where under his dogs.

'Yeah,' she said grimly. 'I tried to cross but the creek doesn't have stones in it.'

His lips twitched. 'How inconsiderate.'

'The last creek did.'

He put his hands up, as if in surrender. 'I cannot tell a lie,' he told her. 'I dropped stones in the first crossing but not this one. The first floods all the time. This one not so much. There's a lot of water coming down. I doubt you'd get back over the first crossing now.'

'You put the stones in…'

'Yes, ma'am.'

She stood and thought about it. She had bare feet—a pair of bright pink sandals had been tossed onto the bank on this side. Obviously she'd waded through first, which was intelligent. Driving into a flooded creek with a sandy base was the opposite.

But now wasn't the time for judging. The water was rising by the minute. 'Would you like me to help you get your car out?'

And any hint of belligerence died. 'Could you? Do you know how?'

'You have cushions on your passenger seat,' he said. He'd been checking out the car while they talked. A big car might be a problem but this looked small enough to push, and with the trac-tion of cushions… 'We could use those.'

'They're Samson's.'

'Samson?'

'My poodle.'

'I see.' He was still having trouble keeping a straight face. 'Is he likely to bite my arm off if I use his cushions?'

She glanced to where Reg and Bluey were still warily circling Samson. Samson was wisely standing still. Very still.

'Your dogs…'

'Are meeting a poodle for the very first time. They won't take a piece out of him, if that's what you're worried about. So Samson won't take a piece out of me if I borrow his cushion?'

'No. Please… If you could…'

'My pleasure, ma'am. I haven't pushed a pink car out of floodwaters for a very long time.'

And then he got bossy.

He swung himself down from his horse. He didn't bother tying it up—the assumption, she guessed, was that it'd stay where he left it and the assumption seemed correct. Then he strode out into the water to her car. He removed the cushions, then stooped and wedged them underwater, in front of the back wheels.

'Rear-wheel drive is useful,' he told her. 'Four-wheel drive is better—it's pretty much essential out here. You didn't think to borrow something a little more useful before driving off-road?'

'This *is* a road.'

'This is a track,' he told her.

He was standing almost thigh-deep in water and he was soaked from pushing the cushions into place.

'I should push,' she offered.

The lips twitched again. 'I'm thinking I might just have a bit more muscle. Could you hop in and switch on the ignition? When I tell you to accelerate, go for it. Straight forward, and as soon as you feel the car get a grip, keep going.'

She thought about it for a moment and saw a problem. A big one. 'Um…'

He paused. 'Um?'

'Are there any more creeks?' she asked, her voice filled with trepidation.

'Any more creeks where?'

'Between here and Malley's Corner.'

'You're headed for Malley's Corner?'

'Yes.' She tilted her chin at the note of incredulity in his voice. It was the same incredulity she'd heard from every one of her family and friends.

He paused for a moment. The water level rose an inch.

'We'll talk about it later,' he said curtly. 'We have minutes to get your car clear before she's properly swamped. Get in and turn it on.'

'But are there more creeks?'

'A dozen or so.'

'Then I can't get to Malley's Corner,' she wailed. 'I need to go back the way I came. Can you push me back to the other side?'

'You want to do a U-turn in the middle of the creek?'

'No, but I don't want to be trapped.'

'I have news for you, lady,' he told her. 'You're already trapped. The only hope we have of getting your car out of this water is to go straight forward and do it now. Get in your car and I'll push or it'll be washed away. Move!'

She gave a yelp of fright—and moved.

She was in such a mess.

Actually, if she was honest, she wasn't in a mess at all. She was perfectly dry. Her little car was on dry land, still drivable. Samson had jumped back up into the passenger seat and was looking around for his cushions. It looked as if she could drive happily away. There were more creeks but for now she was safe.

But she had a cowboy to thank, the guy who'd saved her car—and he was the mess.

Though actually… She *should* be able to describe him as a mess, she thought. He'd shoved the cushions under her back wheels to get traction and then, as she'd touched the accelerator, he'd put his hands under the back of her car and pushed.

She'd felt the strength of him, the sheer muscle. With the acceleration behind him he'd practically heaved the little car free.

She'd stopped and looked back, and her cowboy—her rescuer—was sprawled full length in the water.

When he stood up he almost looked scary. He was seriously big, he was soaked and he was spitting sand. He did not look happy.

When he reached the bank she backed off a little.

'Th…thank you,' she ventured. 'That was very good of you.'

'My pleasure, ma'am,' he said with obvious sarcasm and she winced.

'I'm sorry.'

'All in a day's work. I've heaved stock from bogs before this. Your car's not much bigger than a decent bull.' He wiped away some sand and she had a clearer view of his face. He had deep brown eyes set in a strongly boned face. Strength and capability and toughness was written on every inch of him. This wasn't the sort of guy she ever met in her city life.

'Do you live round here?' she managed and he nodded.

'Over the rise.'

'Then…I guess that means at least you can go home and have a shower. Look, I really am sorry…'

'So what will you do?'

'Go on until I reach the next creek,' she said in a small voice. 'Samson and I can sleep in the car if the water doesn't go down before nightfall. We'll go on tomorrow.'

'Tomorrow…'

'I start work on Tuesday. I guess it's just lucky I left myself a day's leeway.'

Something seemed to be happening on her rescuer's face. There was a tic right next to his jaw. It was sort of…twitching.

Laughter? No. Exasperation?

Maybe.

'You'd better follow me,' he said at last and she blinked.

'Why? I'm sorry; that doesn't sound gracious but you've done enough. Samson and I will be fine.'

'For a fortnight?'

'A fortnight?'

'That's how long they're saying before the flood-waters subside.' He sighed. 'There's been rain all over central New South Wales. It's been dry here, which is why you've been lulled into thinking it's safe to drive, but it's been raining up north like it hasn't for years. The water's pouring into the Murray catchment and all that water's making its way downstream. Creeks that haven't seen water for years are starting to fill. If you'd followed the main road you might have made it…'

'The satnav lady said this way was much shorter,' she said in a small voice.

'Then the satnav lady's a moron,' he said bluntly. 'There's no way you'll get this little car through to Malley's Corner and there's no way you can get back. You're stuck right here and you're stuck for a while.'

She stood and stared at him and he gazed right back. He was looking at her as if she were some sort of strange species.

An idiot.

All her careful plans. All her defiance...

This was just what her father expected—Penelope being stupid once again.

She thought of the last appalling tabloid article she'd read before she'd packed and left—her father explaining to the media why the man who'd intended to marry Penny was now marrying Penny's older half-sister, the gorgeous, clever, talented Felicity.

'They're a much more suitable match,' George had told the journalist. *'Brett is one in a million. He's an employee who's going places and he needs a woman of class to support that. My younger daughter means well, but she's much more interested in her cakes than in taking care of her man. I'm not sure why we all didn't see this was a more sensible match to begin with.'*

Sensible. Right.

She shook herself, shoving painful memories harshly behind her. No, she wouldn't be calling her father for help.

'Is there somewhere I can stay?' she asked in a small voice.

'You're on my land,' he told her. 'From here until the next two creek crossings there's nowhere but Jindalee.'

'Jindalee?'

'My home.'

'Oh.'

She looked at his horse and her mind was twisting so much she even thought of offering to buy the thing and ride off into the sunset. Fording rivers on horseback with Samson riding up front.

Um...not. Even if she could ride a horse. Even if she was game to go near it.

'Do you...do you have a four-wheel drive?' she asked. 'Is it possible that a truck or something could get through?'

'It might,' he said grudgingly.

She'd been trying to figure a way out, but she thought she saw one. 'Could you take me on to Malley's? If you have a truck that can get through we could make it. I could leave my car here and get someone to bring me back to collect it when the water goes down.'

And this is my last chance, she thought desperately, looking into his impassive face. *Please.*

He gazed at her and she forced herself to meet his gaze calmly, as if her request was totally reasonable—as if asking him to drive for at least four hours over flooded creeks was as minor as hiring a cab.

'I can pay,' she added. 'I mean…I can pay well. Like a good day's wages…'

'You have no idea,' he said and then there was even more silence. Was he considering it?

But finally he shook his head.

'It's impossible,' he told her. 'I can't leave the property. I have a team ready to start shearing at dawn and two thousand sheep to be shorn. Nothing's messing with that.'

'You could…maybe come back tonight?'

'In your dreams. The water's coming up. I could end up trapped at Malley's Corner with you. I can't risk sending a couple of my men because I need everyone. So I don't seem to have a choice and neither do you.' He sighed. 'We might as well make the best of it. I'm inviting you home. You and your dog. As long as you don't get in the way of my shearing team, you're welcome to stay at Jindalee for as long as the floodwater takes to recede.'

CHAPTER TWO

PENNY DROVE, SLOWLY and carefully, along the rutted track. He followed behind on his horse, his dogs trotting beside him, and she was aware of him every inch of the way.

He could be an axe murderer. He was sodden and filthy. His jet-black hair was still dripping and his dark face looked grim.

He'd laughed when he first saw her but now he looked as if he'd just been handed a problem and he didn't like it.

She didn't even know his name.

He didn't know hers, she reminded herself. He was opening his house to her, and all he knew about her was that she was dumb enough to get herself stranded in the middle of nowhere. She could be the axe murderer.

She had knives. She thought fleetingly of her precious set, wrapped carefully in one of her crates. They were always super sharp.

What sort of knives did axe murderers use?

'They use axes, idiot,' she said aloud and that was a mistake. The guy on the horse swivelled and stared.

'Axes?' he said cautiously, and she thought, *He'll be thinking he has a real fruitcake here.*

That was what she felt like. A fruitcake.

'Sorry. Um…just thinking of what I'd need if… I mean, if I was stuck camping and needed something like wood to light a fire. I'd need an axe.'

'Right,' he said, still more cautiously. 'But you don't have one?'

'No.'

'You seem to have everything else.'

'I'm going to Malley's to work. I need stuff.'

'You're working at Malley's?' He sounded incredulous. 'That place is a dump.'

'The owner has plans,' she said with as much dignity as she could muster. 'I'm employed to help.'

'It could use a bit of interior decorating,' he agreed. 'From the ground up.' His lips suddenly twitched again. 'And you always carry a teapot?'

'They might only use tea bags.'

'You don't like tea bags?'

'I drink lapsang souchong and it doesn't work in tea bags. I love its smoky flavour. Don't you?'

'Doesn't everyone?' he asked and suddenly he grinned. 'I'm Matt,' he told her. 'Matt Fraser. I'm the owner of Jindalee but I hope you brought your own lapsang souchong with you. Sadly I seem to be short on essentials.'

'I have a year's supply,' she told him and his grin widened.

'Of course you do. And you are?'

'Penelope Hindmarsh-Firth.' He was laughing at

her but she could take it, she decided. She should be used to people laughing at her by now. 'And I'm the owner of one pink car and one white poodle.'

'And a teapot,' he reminded her.

'Thank you. Yes.' She concentrated on negotiating an extra deep rut in the road.

'Penelope...' Matt said as the road levelled again.

'Penny.'

'Penny,' he repeated. 'Did you say Hindmarsh-Firth?'

And her heart sank. He knows, she thought, but there was no sense denying it.

'Yes.'

'Of the Hindmarsh-Firth Corporation?'

'I don't work for them.' Not any more. She said it almost defiantly.

'But you're connected.'

'I might be.'

'The way I heard it,' he said slowly, seemingly thinking as he spoke, 'is that George Hindmarsh, up-and-coming investment banker, married Louise Firth, only daughter of a mining magnate worth billions. Hindmarsh-Firth is now a financial empire that has tentacles worldwide. You're part of that Hindmarsh-Firth family?'

'They could be my parents,' she muttered. 'But I'm still not part of it.'

'I see.'

He didn't, she thought. He couldn't. He'd have

no idea of what it was like growing up in that gold-fish bowl, with her father's ego. He'd have no idea why she'd finally had to run.

'So if I rang up the newspapers now and said I've just pulled a woman called Penelope Hindmarsh-Firth out of a creek, they wouldn't be interested?'

No! 'Please don't,' she whispered and then repeated it, louder, so she was sure he could hear. She was suddenly very close to tears.

'I won't,' he told her, his voice suddenly softening. 'Believe me, I have no wish for media choppers to be circling. Though…'

'Though what?'

'There's someone I need to get here,' he told her. 'It'd almost be worth it—I could tell them they could find you here as long as they brought Pete with them.'

'Pete?'

She hit a bump. The car jolted and the teapot bounced and clanged against the pots underneath it.

'It doesn't matter,' he said roughly. 'I won't do it. I can understand your situation might well cause humiliation. I assume you're heading to Malley's to get out of the spotlight?'

'Yes,' she said and could have wept with gratitude.

'Then you've come to the right place,' he told her. 'And this is a lot cleaner than Malley's. Jindalee has plenty of spare bedrooms, though most are in desperate need of a good dust. As long as you and Samson keep out of my way, you're welcome to hunker down for as long as the flood lasts.'

And then they topped the last rise before the house and Penny was so astounded she stalled the car.

The rain clouds up north must have visited here a while back because the pastures were lush and green. The property was vast and undulating. There were low hills rolling away as far as the eye could see. The land was dotted with stands of magnificent gums. She could see the occasional flock of sheep in the distance, white against green.

But the house… It took her breath away.

It was a real homestead, built a hundred or more years ago. It sat on a slight rise, huge, long and low, built of whitewashed stone. French windows opened to the vast verandas and soft white curtains fluttered out into the warm afternoon breeze. Grapevines massed under the veranda and massive old settees sat under their shade. An ancient dog lay on the top step by the front door as if he was guarding the garden.

And what a garden. It looked almost like an oasis in the middle of this vast grazing property. Even from here she could see the work, the care…

Wisteria hung from massive beamed walkways. She could see rockwork, the same sandstone that lined the creeks, used to merge levels into each other. Bougainvillea, salvia, honeysuckle… Massive trees that looked hundreds of years old. A rock pool with a waterfall that looked almost natural. Roses, roses and more roses.

And birds. As they approached the house a flock of crimson rosellas rose screeching from the gums, wheeling above their heads as if to get a better look, and then settled again.

For why wouldn't they settle? This place looked like paradise.

'Oh, my…' She slowed to a halt. She needed to stop and take it all in.

And Matt pulled his horse to a halt as well. He sat watching her.

'This is… Oh…' She could hardly speak.

'Home,' Matt said and she could feel the love in his voice. And suddenly every doubt about staying here went out of the window.

He loved this place. He loved this garden and surely no one who loved as much as this could be an axe murderer?

'Who does this?' she stammered. She'd tried gardening in the past. It had been a thankless task as her parents moved from prestige property to prestige property, but she knew enough to know that such a seemingly casual, natural garden represented more hard work than she could imagine. 'Your wife?' she asked. 'Or…'

'I don't have a wife,' he said, suddenly curt, and

she thought instinctively that there was a story there. 'But I do have someone helping me in the garden. Donald loves it as much as I do. He's in his eighties now but he won't slow down.'

'Your dad? Grandpa?'

'No.' Once more his reply was curt and she knew suddenly that she needed to back off. This guy wasn't into personal interrogation. 'Donald owned this place before I bought it. He's stayed on because of the garden.'

'That's lovely,' she breathed.

'It is,' he said and he wasn't talking of Donald. His eyes skimmed the house, the garden, the country around them and she saw his face soften. 'There's nowhere I'd rather be.'

She gazed around her, at the low lying hills, at the rich pasture, at the massive gum trees, at the sheer age and beauty of the homestead which seemed to nestle into its surroundings as if it had grown there. 'How much of this do you own?' she breathed.

'As far as you can see and more.' It was impossible for him to hide the pride in his voice.

'Oh, wow!' The property must be vast. She sat and soaked it in, and something in her settled. Who could be fearful or even heartbroken in a place like this?

Okay, she was still heartbroken but maybe she could put it aside.

'What's the building over there?' A low shed

built of ancient handmade bricks sat under the gum trees in the distance. It looked so old it practically disappeared into the landscape.

'That's the shearing shed. The shearers' quarters are behind that.'

And suddenly she was diverted from the farm's beauty.

'There's a dozen trucks. At least.'

'They belong to the shearing team. We start at dawn. You'll need to keep out of the way.'

'Oh, but…' Surely with so many…

'No,' he said, seeing where she was heading and cutting her off before she got started. 'No one's driving you anywhere. You'll find an empty garage around the back. I need to take care of Nugget and talk to the men before I come in for the night, but the back door's open. Put the kettle on and make yourself a cup of…what was it? Lapsang souchong. I'll see you in an hour or so. Meanwhile, welcome to Jindalee, Miss Hindmarsh-Firth. Welcome to my home.'

Matt led Nugget into the stables, unstrapped his gear and started brushing. Nugget looked vaguely surprised. Knowing shearing was about to start, knowing life was about to get crazy, he'd given him a decent brush this morning. But two brushes in one day wouldn't hurt and it might help get his head together.

In one sense the worsening flood was a blessing. The shearing team hadn't listened to the weather forecast. They'd come straight from a property south of here this morning, and there'd been no hint of the flooding to come. That meant when they woke tomorrow and found he had no shearers' cook they couldn't leave in disgust. At least his sheep would be shorn.

But he was facing two weeks of disgruntled shearers. Plus two weeks of a society princess who asked questions.

Penelope Hindmarsh-Firth...

He took his phone from the waterproof protector he always used—thank heaven he'd had it today—and hit the Internet. Thank heaven for satellites too, he thought, glancing at the dish on the top of the house. If he'd used the Internet to good effect he could have tracked the speed of the flooding. He could have let the shearers know not to come, but he'd gambled. He'd known the water was on its way but he'd thought they'd be able to get through this morning. They had. He had two weeks' work for them and a decent amount of supplies.

He'd also thought his cook could get through, but he'd been coming from another property in a different direction. And that had spelled disaster.

First World problem—shearers having to cook their own tucker? Maybe it was, but from time immemorial shearers had counted the quality of food and accommodation as a major enticement. This was a crack team and they expected the best. They couldn't blame him but it would be a sullen two weeks.

'So what are the odds of Miss Hindmarsh-Firth being able to cook?' he asked Nugget and thought of the teapot and grimaced. He needed to know more about the blonde and her white poodle. He leaned back on his horse's hindquarters and Nugget nibbled his ear while he searched *Penelope Hindmarsh-Firth* in his Internet browser.

And what sprang up were gossip columns—a list of them, longer than his screen. Current gossip.

'*Is one Hindmarsh-Firth as good as another?*' '*Sister Swap!*' '*Taggart's gamble pays off...*'

Bemused, he hit the first and read.

Brett Taggart, chief accountant to investment banker George Hindmarsh and heiress Louise Firth, has played a risky hand and won. He wooed the pair's daughter, company PR assistant Penelope, with what we hope were honourable intentions... Familiarity, however, meant a change of direction for our dubiously intentioned Brett. As he was welcomed into the golden world of the Hindmarsh-Firth family, his attention was obviously caught by his fiancée's older half-sister, glamorous social butterfly Felicity. Never let a promise get in the way of a good time, seems to be Brett's philosophy, and rumour has it that he and Felicity might be expecting a Happy Event in the next few months.

Such a ruckus in the family might have some parents casting children out. 'Never darken our door again!' would have been this columnist's reaction to such a back-stabbing sibling, but George and Louise seem to have taken the situation in their stride. In a recent tabloid interview George even insinuated he understands why Brett would choose the gorgeous Felicity over her dumpy, media-shy sister, and Louise refuses to comment. So one wedding has been swapped for another.

Ugh, Matt thought, feeling a wave of sympathy for the 'dumpy, media-shy' Penny.

And then he thought…*dumpy?* What a description for those curves.

Um…let's not go there. He didn't need distraction.

He did not need anyone—except a shearer's cook.

'At least she can make her own tea,' he muttered to Nugget. 'There's a bonus. I wonder if she can make her own toast?'

Penny ventured in through the back door and was met by silence. Samson sniffed forward so she cautiously opened a few doors. The house was a beautiful…mausoleum?

It looked like a magnificent homestead built for a family of a dozen or so, with entertaining on a lavish scale. But it also looked like it hadn't been used for years. The massive sitting room off the main entrance was covered in dust sheets, as were the two other rooms she ventured into. She peeked under the dust sheets and saw furniture that'd look at home in an antique store. An expensive antique store.

There was a small sun-drenched den that looked well used. It was crammed with farming journals, books, a computer, dog beds. Matt's study? A wide passage led to what must be the bedroom wing but she wasn't game to go there.

Feeling more and more like an intruder, she retreated to the kitchen.

Which was…spectacular.

Windows opened to the veranda, to the shearing shed in the distance and to the hills beyond. Sunbeams were dancing on the floor, the ancient timbers worn by years of use. A battered wooden table ran almost the full length of the room, with scattered mismatched chairs that looked incredibly inviting. A small, slow combustion stove stood to one side of an old hearth, as if a far bigger wood stove had been removed. Beside it was a vast industrial oven and cooktop. It looked as if it could feed a small army.

How many people lived here? Hardly anyone by the look of the closed-up rooms, but these ovens… *Wow!*

She glanced again at the firestove. It was lit and emitting a gentle warmth. She'd never used one. Could she make bread?

What was she thinking of? Baking?

This situation was a mess. She didn't want to be here and Matt Fraser didn't want her here. Her job at Malley's Corner was in doubt. She'd ring them now but would they still want her when she arrived two weeks late?

She was stuck here for two weeks, with a man she didn't know.

But she was suddenly thinking: did he have decent flour?

There was a door to the side which looked like it could lead to a pantry. She shouldn't pry. The very stillness of the house was making her nervous, but he'd said she could make herself a cup of tea.

She did have tea but it was packed at the bottom of one of her crates. So she needed to check the pantry…

She opened the pantry door and gasped.

This pantry was huge, and it was stocked as if Matt was expecting to feed an army.

There were flour bins, big ones, topped to overflowing. There were bins of rice, of sugar. There were mountains of cans, stacks of packs of pasta. There was every dried herb and sauce she could imagine.

There were two vast refrigerators and freezers, and another door led to a coolroom. She saw vegetables, fruit, every perishable a cook could need. There were whole sides of beef and lamb. Who could eat this much meat?

The shearing team? She'd read descriptions of life on the big sheep stations. Gun shearers, working twelve-hour days, pushing themselves to the limits, while the farmer's wife pushed herself to the limit feeding them.

Matt had no wife. There was no evidence of a housekeeper.

Was he planning to cook, or did one of those trucks out there belong to a cook?

She closed the lid of the freezer and saw an enormous list pinned to the wall. It was an inventory of everything she'd just seen.

It was printed out as an email. She flicked through to the end.

Can you get all this in stock and have it waiting? I'll be there on the seventh by mid-afternoon, but my first cook will be smoko on the eighth. See you then.

So he did have a cook. He'd probably be over with the men now, she thought. Maybe Matt was there too. Maybe they were sitting round drinking beer while Matt told them about the dopey blonde he'd pulled out of the water.

And suddenly all the fears of the past few weeks crowded back.

She was stuck in the middle of nowhere, where no one wanted her. She was stuck for two weeks.

A shearer's cook would be taking over this kitchen from tomorrow morning. Maybe she could help, she thought, but she'd worked in enough kitchens to know how possessive cooks could be.

'I might be allowed to wash dishes,' she told Samson morosely.

She found a tea bag—actually, she found about a thousand tea bags. They weren't generic, but they weren't lapsang souchong either.

'We'll have to slum it,' she told her dog, and made her tea and headed out to the veranda.

The big, old collie she'd seen earlier was still snoozing on the step. He raised his head and gave his tail a faint wag, then settled back down to the serious business of sleeping.

An old man was dead-heading roses. He was stooped and weathered with age, almost a part of the land around him. He glanced up from his roses as she emerged from the back door, and startled as if he'd just seen a ghost.

'Hi,' Penny called. 'I'm Penny.'

He didn't answer. Instead he dropped the canvas bag he'd been carrying and backed away. Ghosts, it seemed, were scary.

Penny sighed. She plonked herself down on the edge of the veranda and gazed out over the garden to the rolling plains beyond. Samson eyed the old dog warily, and then plonked down beside her.

'This is a beautiful view,' she told Samson. 'But I might just get sick of it after two weeks.'

Samson put his nose into the crook of her arm and whined. Samson, it seemed, was in complete agreement.

To say the men were unhappy would be an understatement.

'So who's going to cook?' Bert, self-proclaimed shearers' foreman, sounded incredulous.

'Me,' Matt told him. 'It means I can't spend much time in the shed, but Ron and Harv will have things under control.' Ron was his right-hand man, Harv his jackeroo. They were both capable sheep men.

Leaving the shed in their hands was still a risk. Half the trick of a smooth shear was the owner being hands-on. Men worked at full capacity, day after day, pushing themselves to the limit because the sooner they finished the sooner they'd be paid, and that was a recipe for problems. Tensions escalated fast. Ron and Harv were both men who disliked conflict and backed away from it—there was a reason they both worked on such an isolated property. Matt didn't like conflict either, but he could deal. He had the authority to dock wages, to kick a drunk shearer off the team or, worse, to recommend to other station owners which teams not to employ.

But Ron and Harv couldn't cook to save their lives. They lived on a diet of corned beef, beer and the occasional apple to prevent scurvy. At least Matt could do a decent spag. bol.

He had no choice. The kitchen was his.

'So we'll be eating pasta and boiled beef for two weeks?' Bert demanded and Matt shrugged.

'I'll do my best. Sorry, guys. I'm as unhappy about this as you are.'

'So what about the Sheila we just saw you drive in with?' Bert demanded. 'Have you replaced Pete with a bit of fluff?'

'I haven't. She was stuck in the creek and I pulled her out. She's stuck here too and, before you ask, I suspect she might be able to brew a decent tea but not much else.'

'Great,' Bert growled. 'That's just great.'

'Sorry,' Matt told him. 'But that's the situation and we're stuck with it.'

And also a cute blonde with curves?

Do not go there. What was wrong with him? That was the second time he'd thought it.

Two weeks...

Stay well clear, he told himself. The last thing he needed was yet another woman complicating his life.

CHAPTER THREE

MATT RETURNED TO FIND Penny on the veranda, trying to make friends with Donald's dog. He greeted her curtly. There was a lot to be done before he could sleep. If she was expecting to be entertained he might as well make things clear now.

He showed her which bedroom she could use. It was big, it overlooked the garden and it had the extra advantage of being as far away from his as possible. Plus it had its own bathroom. For a Hindmarsh-Firth it might still be slumming it, he thought, but it'd be a thousand times better than the accommodation she'd get at Malley's Corner.

What on earth was she intending to do at Malley's? He'd ask some time, he thought, but he had to be up before dawn to make sure the first mob was ready to go, he had to check the sheep again tonight and he needed to eat.

But he should offer to feed her, he decided. From tomorrow he was faced with feeding the multitude. He might as well start now.

'Dinner's in half an hour,' he told her as he dumped her gear in her bedroom—how much stuff could one woman use? 'At seven.'

'I can help.' She hesitated. 'I'd like to.'

'I'll do it.' He wanted to eat and run, not sit while she fussed over something fancy. 'Thirty minutes. Kitchen. Oh, and there's dog food…'

'Samson has his own dog food.'

'Of course he does,' he said shortly and left her to her unpacking.

Showered, clean of the river sand, he felt better but not much. He tossed bacon and tomatoes into a frying pan, put bread in the toaster and set plates on the table.

Right on seven she walked in the door. She'd changed too. She'd obviously showered as well, for her curls were still damp. She was wearing jeans and a T-shirt and she'd caught her curls back in a ponytail.

He glanced around as she came into the room and had to force himself to turn back to the frying pan.

She looked fresh and clean and…cute? More than cute.

Curvy? Bouncy?

Sexy.

Cut it out, he told himself and concentrated on the bacon.

'The house is lovely,' she told him. 'Thank you for taking me in.'

'It's not like I had a choice.' He thought about that for a moment and decided he sounded a bore. 'Sorry. You're welcome. And yes, it's lovely. Eggs?'

Then he figured as a conversational gambit it needed a little extra. 'How many?'

'Two, please.' Her feet were bare. She padded over to the bench beside the firestove and hauled herself up so her legs were swinging. 'You can fry on this? I've never used a slow combustion stove.'

'It's a skill,' he said, deciding to sound modest.

'What else can you do on it?'

Uh oh. She'd called him out. He grinned and cracked an egg into the pan. 'Sausages,' he told her. 'And I can boil stuff.'

'So you use the big oven?'

'Not usually. The firestove suits me. If it's a cold morning I put my boots in the oven. Oh, and the occasional live lamb.'

'You put lambs in the oven?'

'It's the best place for a lamb that's been caught in the frost,' he told her. 'I can fit a lamb and boots in there all at once. Lamb and boots come out warm and ready to go. It's a win-win for everyone. Who needs an oven for baking?'

'But you can still bake in it?'

'I could try,' he told her. 'But anything I put in there might come out smelling of wet wool and boot leather.'

'Yum,' she said and then looked down at his frying eggs. 'Don't let them get hard.'

'What?' He stared down at the five eggs he'd cracked. He picked up the egg slice to flip them but Penny put her hand out and held his. Stopping him mid-flip.

'You want runny yolks?'

'I don't mind.'

'Runny's nicer.'

'Yeah, but…'

'Just spoon a little hot fat over them. It's much less likely to burst the yolks.'

'I don't have time for nice.'

'Then let me,' she told him and jumped down, grabbed a spoon and edged him out of the way.

Her body hit his and all of a sudden they were close. Too close.

He felt… He didn't know what he felt. How long since he'd stood beside a woman in a kitchen?

This was not a sensation he needed to be feeling tonight.

He edged away fast, and stood and watched while she carefully spooned hot fat over the yolks.

'Done,' she said.

She flicked bacon and tomatoes he'd fried earlier onto the toast and then carefully slid the eggs on top.

How had she done that? It was weird but somehow she'd made it look…sort of gourmet? When he piled eggs and bacon onto a plate they looked like eggs and bacon. She'd sort of set the tomatoes at one side and then made a round of bacon. The eggs slid on top and it looked…great.

He'd been hungry. Now he was even hungrier.

And so, it seemed, was she. She sat down and tackled her eggs and bacon as if she hadn't seen food in a week. She was enjoying every mouthful of this very plain meal.

He thought of the few women he knew and the way they ate. Not like this. This was almost sensual.

'Wow,' she breathed as she finished her first egg and tackled her bacon. 'Yum!'

'It's all in the cooking,' he said and she grinned. It was a great grin, he decided. Kind of endearing.

'Yeah, great fat scooping.' She shook her head. 'Nope. These eggs… This bacon…'

'Home grown,' he told her. 'They're Donald's projects.'

'Donald?'

'I told you about him. He used to own this property. He got too old to run it; he sold it but the thought of leaving broke his heart. I offered him one of the shearers' cottages in return for keeping up the garden. He's been with me for ten years now, running a few of his precious pigs, caring for his hens and keeping my garden magnificent. Win-win for everyone.'

'Are the eggs free range too?' she asked.

'We lock 'em up at night. Which reminds me…' He headed for the sink, dumping his dishes. 'I need to go. Sleep well. Anything you need in the morning, help yourself. I'll be gone before dawn.'

'You start shearing before dawn?'

'The pens are already full for the dawn start but I'll run the south mob into the home paddock to refill the pens as the men work. But I'll be back here by about nine to make sandwiches.'

'*You're* making sandwiches?'

'Yeah.' He grimaced. 'That's all they're getting. But it doesn't affect you. Just stay away from the sheds, that's all I ask. I don't like distractions.'

'I'm a distraction?'

He turned and looked at her. *Cute*, he thought again. *Definitely cute.*

Her poodle was at her feet. Most of the shearers had dogs.

Penny and Samson in the shearers' shed? No and no and no.

'Definitely a distraction. Stay away,' he growled, possibly more gruffly than he intended.

But she looked distracted now. She was frowning. 'You're making sandwiches?' she said again.

'Yes.'

'And you just said all you can do is sausages and boiling stuff.'

'I'll boil a couple of slabs of beef for lunch.'

The thought of it was almost overwhelming but who else would do it? Ron and Harv could be depended on to keep the sheep coming in and

clear the pens but their cooking skills were zero.
Donald was eighty-seven. That was his pool of
workers.

He could imagine the reaction of the shearers if
he went over there now and said: *Hey, do any of
you cook? Care to swap jobs?*

But he was eyeing the woman at the table with
caution. She'd known how to cook an egg. That
was about twenty per cent of his cooking skill.
Maybe…

But she drove a pink car. She had a poodle. She
came from one of the richest families in Australia.

Ask.

'I employ a shearers' cook,' he told her. 'The
best. Pete sent me lists. I have everything I need—
except Pete. He's stuck on the far side of the floodwater.' He hesitated. 'So I'm stuck with cooking.
But any help you could give me…'

'I'll cook.'

Silence.

I'll cook.

Two magic words.

'You can cook?'

'Don't sound so shocked. Why do you think I
was heading for Malley's Corner?'

'You were going to Malley's to *cook*?' He
couldn't keep the incredulity from his voice.

'What's wrong with that?' She glared. 'Just because my family's…'

'The richest family in Australia?'

'We're not. There are mining magnates richer than us.'

'Of course there are.'

'Don't be sarcastic. Besides, this has nothing to do with money. Though…' she considered '…I'm stuck here so I might as well make myself useful. Consider it payment for board.'

'Do you have any idea how hard it is to cook for a shearers' team?'

'You were going to do it.'

'Now you sound sarcastic.'

And she grinned. 'I do,' she conceded. 'But I can do better than sandwiches.'

'We have a team of twenty shearers, classers and roustabouts. Do you have any idea how much they eat?'

'I've cooked for hundreds.'

'*You…*'

'You say that like I'm some sort of amoebic slug,' she said carefully. 'Why shouldn't I cook? Why do you think Malley hired me?'

'Malley would employ anyone with a pulse. Come to think of it, rumour was that his last cook didn't have one.'

'Then he's about to be surprised. I even have qualifications.'

'You're kidding.'

'Only a basic apprenticeship,' she admitted. 'But

I've done lots of cooking classes in amazing places. Mum and Dad approved of those.'

'I just read an article online,' he told her. A man had to be careful but he might as well say it. Not that he had a recruitment pool of hundreds but he needed to know what he was getting into. 'It described you as a PR assistant in your family corporation. It also said you were nursing a bruised ego and a broken heart.'

She froze. 'You checked up on me.'

'I did. About the broken heart bit. Your sister… I'm sorry…'

And all of a sudden the apologetic, polite blonde was transformed by temper.

'Don't you dare go there,' she snapped. 'I don't want sorry. Every one of my so-called friends are sorry, but not sorry enough to refuse an invitation to the massive wedding my parents are organizing right now. My father says a big function's important to show there's no family rift. So there's no family rift. Business as usual.'

He winced. 'That must hurt. Every major tabloid…'

'Is enjoying it very much.' She cut him off bitterly. 'But that's important how? Right now I'm offering to cook for you. Isn't there a Discrimination Act somewhere that says asking employees about their past appalling taste in men is illegal?'

'Are you applying for a job?'

'I might be,' she snapped. 'As long as you don't rake up my family. I've left them in Sydney and that's where they're staying. I like the fact that half of Australia is flooding between here and there. Do you like the fact that I can cook?'

There was no arguing with that. 'Yes.'

'So let's move on. Your shearers like sandwiches? Are you any better at making them than frying eggs?'

'Mine would be pretty basic sandwiches,' he admitted.

The grandfather clock in the hallway chimed eight. He should be gone, he thought. There was so much to do before dark.

But he had the offer of a cook.

She intrigued him. She was half perky, half defensive.

It sounded as if her family had cut her a raw deal and he'd seen enough of the tabloids to realize how widely her humiliation must have spread. She must be hurting a lot under her pink bravado.

What he wanted was to probe deeper into what was behind her blind run to Malley's. But then... this was personal and hadn't he learned a long time ago not to get personal with women? The last thing he needed was a wealthy blonde socialite sobbing on his chest while she spilt all.

And she was right. Her past had no bearing on her ability to cook.

She could probably only do fancy, he thought. Soufflés and caviar and truffles. But she *had* cooked a mean egg, which was more than he could do. And how could her cooking be worse than his efforts?

'If you really could...'

'I could try,' she told him, her glare fading. She looked as if she was sensing his train of thought. 'You can sack me if it doesn't work.' She smiled suddenly, and he thought she had a great smile. It lit her face.

It lit the room.

'Tell me what you need,' she said and he had to force himself to focus on something that wasn't that smile.

'Morning smoko, dinner and arvo tea. The shearers make their own breakfast and evening meal, but our dinner's midday, when we need a full, hot meal to keep going. You have no idea how many calories a gun shearer burns. Are you really serious about helping?'

'I'm serious.'

'Okay.' He took a deep breath, seeing clear air where from the time he'd had the call from Pete he'd only seen fog. 'At ten you'd provide smoko— morning tea. You'd bring the food over to the shed. I'll come and help you carry it. Then at twelve-thirty they all come here for a buffet dinner and take it onto the veranda to eat. At three it's time for arvo tea and you take that to the shed as well. It saves time. You'd be expected to cook a couple of extra roasts and leave them in the shearer's quarters so they can use that as a base for their evening meal.'

'Wow,' she said and looked at the big stove. 'No wonder you have three ovens. Is there an instruction manual?'

'On the Internet.'

'You have Internet?'

'Yep. Satellite. I'll give you the password.'

She stood up and her smile widened until the defensiveness of moments ago disappeared entirely.

'You have no idea how good that makes me feel,' she told him. 'Half an hour ago I was trapped in the middle of nowhere feeling useless. Now I have a job and Internet and there's nothing more I need in the world. Right. You'd better put those chooks to bed and gather those sheep or whatever you have to do. Leave me be, Matt. I'm about to get busy.'

He'd been dismissed.

She was needed! She stood in the great kitchen and, for the first time since that appalling night when Brett and Felicity had appeared at the family dinner table hand in hand and smugly announced the new order of things, she felt as if she was standing on firm ground again.

A shearing team of twenty. Two weeks' hard work, she thought with satisfaction. Two weeks when she could put her head down and forget that every tabloid in the country was running articles pitying her.

She'd be working for Matt.

Matt…

And suddenly her thoughts went off at a tangent. Matt. The way he'd said he was sorry. He'd said it…as if he understood. How was that possible? It had been a throwaway line, a platitude, something that had been said to her over and over before her family and her friends had moved on to the new normal.

But his eyes were kind.

And the rest of him…

Wow.

And that was enough to make her give herself a fast mental slap to the side of the head. What was she thinking? He was her new boss. He was the owner of this place, a guy who lived and breathed the land, a guy who'd practically lifted her car and heaved it out of the water.

She'd been brought up with suits. She'd never met anyone even vaguely like Matt.

He made her feel…breathless.

Oh, for heaven's sake. It had been less than a month since she'd been unceremoniously dumped by Brett. She'd thought she was in love, and look how that had turned out.

'I have no sense at all,' she told Samson. 'Okay, he might be good-looking enough to make my toes curl but my toes are not a good indicator. My father thinks I'm an idiot, and where men are concerned I've just proved him spectacularly right. I need to ignore Matt Fraser and get on with my job.'

She opened the pantry again and gazed at the contents in delight.

This place was like a miniature supermarket. Filled with hope, she headed out the back. A vegetable garden! Herbs!

Her head was spinning in all directions. What first?

She could make cupcakes for morning tea. No. She pulled herself up short. Cupcakes might seem girly and the last thing she needed was guys thinking her food was girly. Okay, lamingtons. Better. She could whip up a couple of sponges now and coat them first thing in the morning. Then maybe a couple of big frittatas for lunch, with salads from the gorgeous stuff in the garden and fresh crusty bread. She had an overnight bread recipe. She could start it now so it'd rise magnificently overnight.

She looked at the sacks of flour and realized that Matt had supplies for an army. This must be provisioning for the rest of the year.

She wasn't complaining.

Next? What had Matt called it…arvo tea? If they'd eaten a big lunch they wouldn't want much. Chocolate brownies?

'Let's go,' she told Samson and he wiggled his tail at the joy in her voice.

There hadn't been much joy lately but she was feeling it now.

And she had to ask herself—was it just a little bit because a guy called Matt Fraser would be sharing a house with her for the next two weeks?

Was it just a little bit because a guy called Matt Fraser had caused a tingle of something she couldn't put a name to?

'It has nothing to do with Matt,' she told Samson severely. 'It's only the fact that I'm a world away from ghastly Brett and smug Felicity, and I'm needed.'

And the fact that Matt was sexy as…

Surely that had nothing to do with anything at all?

He'd met her only hours before. She was a society princess in a pink car and she had nothing to do with his world.

So why was he still feeling her hand on his, the way her body had seemed to melt into his as she'd edged him aside to stop him doing the unthinkable—flipping his eggs!

Why did it suddenly feel as if his world was tilting?

There was no reason at all, he told himself and headed out to make sure the hens were locked up for the night.

'Who is she?' It was Donald—caring for the chooks was his job. But increasingly Donald forgot. Age was beginning to fuddle him, but he didn't seem to notice that Matt double-checked on most things he did.

Donald had run this property alone for fifty years. He was a confirmed bachelor and to say he treated women as aliens would be an understatement. Penny's presence, it seemed, had shocked him to the core.

'I pulled her out of the creek,' Matt told him. 'She was taking a dumb shortcut. She's stuck here until the water goes down.'

'Stuck. Here.' Donald said the two words as if they might explode and Matt almost laughed. He thought of the ditzy little blonde in his kitchen and wondered if there was anything less scary.

Although there were scary elements. Like the way his body reacted to her.

Um...let's not go there.

'She can cook,' he told Donald as he shooed the last hen into the pen and started collecting the eggs. 'The shearers' cook is stuck on the far side of the floodwater. If she can keep the team happy…'

'She can cook!' Donald's mother had run off with a wool-buyer when Donald was seven. His opinion of women had been set in stone since.

He grinned. 'I hear some women can.'

Donald thought about it. 'Rufus seems to like her,' he conceded at last. 'I watched her scratch his ear so she can't be all bad. What's that bit of fluff she's got with her?'

'A poodle.'

'A poodle at Jindalee! What next?'

'I'm thinking of getting him to help drafting the mobs in the morning,' Matt said and Donald gave a crack of laughter.

'He might end up getting shorn himself. I wonder what the classer'd make of that fleece?' He grinned. 'So you've got a woman and a poodle in the homestead. Want to kip in my place for the duration?'

'That'd be a bit of overkill. I've put her in your old bedroom and you know I sleep at the other end of the house. I think we can manage.'

'Women reel you in.'

'That's eighty years of experience speaking?'

'Eighty years of keeping out of their way. Mark my words, boy, it's like a disease.'

'I've been married, had a kid and have the

scars to prove it,' Matt said, his grin fading. 'I'm immune.'

'No one's immune.' Donald shook his head and gestured to the house with a grimy thumb. 'Don't you go in till she's safely in bed and leave before she wakes up. Have your cornflakes at my place.'

'I'll be careful,' Matt promised him and smiled, although suddenly for some reason he didn't feel like smiling.

He thought of Penny—maybe Donald's advice was wise.

Lifting eggs from the nesting boxes, he enjoyed, as he always did, the warmth, the miracle of their production. He'd never quite got over the miracle of owning this place. Of never being told to move on.

He found himself thinking of his mother, going from one disastrous love affair to another, dragging her son with her. He'd learned early that when his mother fell in love it meant disaster.

She'd left and finally he'd figured he didn't need her.

After that...his first farm, financial security, finally feeling he could look forward.

And then deciding he could love.

Darrilyn.

And there it was again—disaster. Because Darrilyn didn't want him. She wanted the things his money represented. Two minutes after they were married she was pushing him to leave the farm he loved, and when he didn't…

Yeah, well, that was old history now. He didn't need Darrilyn. He didn't need anyone. But Donald was right.

He needed to be careful.

CHAPTER FOUR

THEY LOOKED BEAUTIFUL.

Penny gazed at the table in satisfaction. She had two plates of lamingtons ready to go. She'd rolled her cakes in rich chocolate sauce, coated them in coconut and filled them with cream. She'd thought of the difficulties of plates and spoons over in the yard so she'd gone small, but she'd made two each to compensate.

She'd piled them in beautifully stacked pyramids. They looked exquisite.

But this wasn't a social event, she reminded herself. Two lamingtons might not be enough, so she made a few rounds of club sandwiches, bite-sized beauties. She cut them into four-point serves and set them on a plate in the lamingtons' midst. They looked great.

She glanced at the clock and felt a little swell of pride. She had the ovens hot for the frittatas for lunch. They were almost ready to pop in. She had fifteen minutes before smoko and she was totally in control.

Matt would walk in any minute.

And here he was. He looked filthy, his pants and open neck shirt coated in dust, his boots caked in… whatever, she didn't want to think about it. His face was smeared with dust and his hair plastered down with sweat. 'Hey. Nearly ready?'

She lifted her lamingtons for inspection. 'We can take them over now if you like.'

He glanced at the table and his gaze moved on. 'Where's the rest?'

'The rest?'

There was a pregnant pause. And then… 'This is all there is?'

'Two lamingtons, two points of sandwiches each. How much more…'

He swore and headed for the pantry, leaving a trail of filthy footsteps over her nice, clean kitchen floor.

Her kitchen. That was how she felt when she worked. This was her domain.

Um…not. Matt had flung open the pantry door and was foraging behind the flour sacks. He emerged with three boxes.

Charity sale Christmas cakes. Big ones.

'They hate them but they'll have to do,' he snapped. 'Help me chop them up. They'll stop work in half an hour and if this is all you have…'

'But there's plenty,' she stammered and he gave her a look that resembled—eerily—the one her father gave her all the time. Like: *You've been an idiot but what else could I expect?*

'This isn't your society morning tea,' he snapped,

ripping cartons open. 'It's fuel. Grab a knife and help me.'

She was having trouble moving. This was supposed to be her domain, the kitchen, her food—and he was treating her like an idiot. She felt sick.

A memory came flooding back of the dinner a month ago. She and her parents in the family home, the mansion overlooking Sydney Harbour. It had been her birthday. She'd like a family dinner, she'd told them. Just her parents, her half-sister and her fiancé.

And she'd cooked, because that was what she loved to do. She'd cooked what Brett loved to eat—stylish, with expensive ingredients, the sort of meal her father would enjoy paying a lot of money for in a society restaurant. She'd worked hard but she thought she'd got it right.

She'd even made time to get her hair done and she was wearing a new dress. Flushed with success, she'd only been a little disconcerted when Brett was late. And Felicity... Well, her sister was always late.

And then they'd walked in, hand in hand. *'We're so sorry, Penny, but we have something to tell you...'*

Matt was already slicing the first cake but at her silence he glanced up. Maybe the colour had drained from her face. Maybe she looked how she felt—as if she was about to be sick. For whatever reason, he put the knife down.

'What?'

'I...'

'It's okay,' he told her, obviously making an effort to sound calm. 'They're very nice lamingtons but this isn't a society fund-raiser where everyone's spent the last three hours thinking about what to wear. Some of these guys have shorn forty sheep since they last ate, and they intend to do forty more before their next meal. Calories first, niceties second. Help me, Penny.' And then, as she still didn't move, he added, 'Please.'

And finally her stunned brain shifted back into gear. She shoved away the sour taste of failure that followed her everywhere.

Fuel. Hungry workers who'd been head down since dawn.

Cute little lamingtons? She must have been nuts.

What then? Hot. Filling. Fast.

She had it.

'Ramp the ovens up,' she snapped and headed for the freezer. 'All of them. High as you can go. And then wash your hands. I need help and you're not touching my food with those hands.'

'We don't have time...'

'We'll be ten minutes late. They have a choice of a late smoko or eating your disgusting cake. You choose.'

* * *

He could order her aside and chop up the fruitcake the team despised—or he could trust her.

He went for the second. He cranked up the ovens and headed for the wash house. Two minutes later he was back, clean at least to the elbows.

By the time he returned, Penny had hauled sheets of frozen pastry from the freezer and was separating them onto baking trays.

'Three ovens, six trays,' she muttered. 'Surely that'll feed them.' She indicated jars of pasta sauce on the bench. 'Open them and start spreading,' she told him. 'Not too thick. Go.'

Hang on. He was the boss. This was his house, his kitchen, his shearing team waiting to be fed. The sensible thing was to keep chopping fruitcake but Penny had suddenly transformed from a cute little blonde into a cook with power. With Matt as an underling.

Fascinated, he snagged the first jar and started spreading.

Penny was diving into the coolroom, hauling out mushrooms, salami, mozzarella. She didn't so much as glance at him. She headed to the sink, dumped the mushrooms under the tap and then started ripping open the salami.

'Aren't you supposed to wipe mushrooms?' he managed. To say he was bemused would be an understatement.

'In what universe do we have time to wipe mushrooms?' She hauled out a vast chopping board and, while the tap washed the mushrooms for her, she started on the salami. Her hands were moving so fast the knife was a blur. 'I could leave them unwashed but I have an aversion to dirt.' She gave herself half a second to glance with disgust at his boots. 'Even if you don't. You finished?'

'Almost.' He poured the last jar over the pastry and spread it to the edges. 'Done.'

'Then I want this salami all over them. Rough and thick—we have no time for thin and fancy.' She hauled the mushrooms out of the sink and dumped them on a couple of tea towels, flipping them over with the fabric to get most of the water out. World's fastest wash. 'Back in two seconds. I'm getting herbs.'

And she was gone, only to appear a moment later with a vast bunch of basil. 'Great garden,' she told him, grabbing another chopping board.

He was too stunned to answer.

They chopped side by side. There was no time, no need to talk.

And suddenly Matt found himself thinking this was just like the shearing shed. When things worked, it was like a well-oiled machine. There was a common purpose. There was urgency.

His knife skills weren't up to hers. In fact they were about ten per cent of hers. He didn't mind.

This woman had skills he hadn't even begun to appreciate.

Wow, she was fast.

It was the strangest feeling. To have a woman in his kitchen. To have *this* woman in his kitchen.

She was a society princess with a pink car and a poodle and knife skills that'd do any master chef proud.

Her body brushed his as she turned to fetch more mushrooms and he felt…

Concentrate on salami, he told himself and it was a hard ask.

But three minutes later they had six trays of 'pizza' in the oven.

'The herbs go on when it comes out,' she told him.

'We won't have time to garnish…'

'Nothing goes out of my kitchen unless it's perfect,' she snapped. She glanced at the clock. 'Right, it's nine minutes before ten. This'll take fifteen minutes to cook so I'll be exactly ten minutes late. I hope that's acceptable. Come back at eight minutes past and help me carry it over.'

He almost grinned. He thought of his shearing team. Craig was the expert there, and Matt was wise enough to follow orders. Did he have just such an expert in his kitchen?

'How can it be ready by then?' He must have sounded incredulous because she smiled.

'Are you kidding? I might even have time to powder my nose before I help you take it out there.'

Taking the food over to the shed was an eye-opener.

A campfire had been lit on the side of the shed. There were a couple of trestle tables and a heap of logs serving as seats. Three billies hung from a rod across the fire.

The fire was surrounded by men and women who looked as filthy as Matt—or worse.

One of the men looked up as Penny and Matt approached and gave a shrill, two-fingers-in-the-mouth whistle. 'Ducks on the pond,' he called and everyone stopped what they were doing and stared.

'Hey.' It was hard to tell the women from the men but it was a female voice. 'You idiot, Harry. Ducks on the pond's a stupid way of saying women are near the shed. What about Marg and me?'

'You don't count,' one of the shearers retorted. 'You gotta have t… I mean you gotta have boobs and legs to count. You and Margie might have 'em but they're hidden under sheep dung. Put you in a bikini, we'll give you the respect you deserve.'

'Yeah, classifying us as ducks. Very respectful.' One of the women came forward and took plates from Penny. 'Take no notice of them, sweetheart. I'm Greta, this is Margie and the rest of this lot don't matter. If they had one more neuron between them, it'd be lonely.' She glanced down at the steaming piles of pizza. 'Wow! Great tucker.'

And then there was no more talk at all.

The food disappeared in moments. Penny stood and watched and thought of the two frittatas she had ready to go in the oven.

How long before the next meal?

But Matt had guessed her thoughts. He'd obviously seen the pathetically small frittatas.

'There are a couple of massive hams in the cool room,' he told her. 'We can use your pretty pies as a side dish for cold ham and peas and potatoes. Penny, you saved my butt and I'm grateful, but from now on it doesn't matter if it's not pretty. At this stage we're in survival mode.'

And she glanced up at him and saw...sympathy!

The team had demolished the food and were heading back to the shed. Matt was clearly needing to head back too, but he'd stopped because he needed to reassure her.

He wanted to tell her it was okay to serve cold ham and peas and potatoes.

She thought again of that dinner with her parents, the joy, the certainty that all was right with her world, and then the crashing deflation.

This morning's pizza had been a massive effort. To serve quality food for every single meal would see her exhausted beyond belief.

She *could* serve his horrid cold ham, she thought, but that would be the equivalent of running away, as she'd run away from Sydney. But there was no-where to run now.

She braced her shoulders and took a deep breath, hauling herself up to her whole five feet three. Where were stilettoes when a girl needed them?

'I'll have lun…dinner ready for you at twelve-thirty,' she told him. 'And there won't be a bit of cold ham in sight.'

He should be back in the shed. These guys were fast—they didn't have the reputation of being the best shearing team in South Australia for noth-ing. The mob of sheep waiting in the pens outside was being thinned by the minute. He needed to get more in.

Instead he took a moment to watch her go.

She was stalking back to the house. He could sense indignation in the very way she held her shoulders.

And humiliation.

She'd been proud of her lamingtons.

They were great lamingtons, he conceded. He'd only just managed to snaffle one before they were gone. There was no doubt she could cook.

She'd pulled out a miracle.

He watched as she stopped to greet Donald's dog. She bent and fondled his ears and said something, and for some reason he wanted badly to know what it was.

She was wearing shorts and a T-shirt. Her bouncy curls were caught in a ponytail. The media thing he'd read yesterday said she was twenty-seven but she looked about seventeen.

'Hey, Matt…' It was Harv, yelling from the shed. 'You want to get the next mob in or will I?'

He shook himself. It didn't matter what Penny did or didn't look like. He needed to get to work. He'd have to knock off early to go and make sure she'd sliced enough ham. Could she guess how many spuds she had to cook?

He glanced at her again. She was heading up the veranda. She looked great in those shorts. Totally inappropriate for this setting but great. She'd squared her shoulders and she was walking with a bounce again. Rufus was following and for a weird moment he wouldn't mind doing the same.

Food. Fast. Right.

She stared at her two quiches and three sticks of bread dough doing their final rise in a sunbeam on the window ledge—an entrée for that mob, she thought. A snack.

The reason that pantry was packed… Yeah, she got it.

There were sides of lamb, pork and beef hung on great hooks in the coolroom. Whole sides.

She usually bought lamb boned out and butter-flied, pork belly trimmed to perfection.

But she had done a butchering course. Once upon a time a two star chef who'd agreed to have her help in his kitchen had yelled it at her. 'You want to understand meat, you need to understand the basics.' He hadn't made her kill her own cow but she had handled slabs of meat almost as big as this.

But to cut it into roasts, marinade it, get it into an oven she didn't know...

'Not going to happen,' she muttered. 'But I reckon I could get chops cut and cooked in time. First, let's get the bread divided and pies baked, and then I'm going to tackle me a sheep.'

Matt didn't leave the shed until ten minutes before the team was due to head to the kitchen.

He was running late. With Penny's knife skills though, and now she knew how much they ate, surely she'd have plated enough?

He opened the kitchen door—and the smell lit-erally stopped him in his tracks. He could smell cooked lamb, rich sauces, apple pies redolent with cinnamon and cloves. Fried onions, fried chicken? His senses couldn't take it all in.

He gazed around the kitchen in stupefaction. The warming plate and the top of the damped-down firestove were piled high with loaded dishes, keeping warm. There were rounds of crumbed lamb cutlets, fried chicken, slices of some sort of vegetable quiche that looked amazing. Jugs of steaming sauces. Plates of crusty rolls. A vast bowl of tiny potatoes with butter and parsley. Two—no, make that three—casseroles full of mixed vegetables. Was that a ratatouille?

And to the side there were steaming fruit pies, with great bowls of whipped cream.

'Do you think we still need the ham?' Penny asked demurely and he blinked.

This wasn't the same clean Penny. She was almost as filthy as he was, but in a different way. Flour seemed to be smudged everywhere. A great apricot-coloured smear was splashed down her front. The curls from her ponytail had wisped out of their band and were clinging to her face.

And once again came that thought… She looked adorable.

'I'm a mess,' she told him when he couldn't find the words to speak. 'The team'll be here in five minutes, right? If you want me to serve, I'll go get changed. Everything's ready.'

And it was. The team would think they'd died and gone to heaven.

'Or do you want me to disappear?' Penny added. 'Ducks on the pond, hey?'

'Ducks is a sexist label,' he told her. 'Harry's old school—Margie and Greta have spent the last couple of hours lecturing him on respect.' He grinned. 'But, speaking of respect… You, Penelope Hindmarsh-Firth, are a proper shearer's cook and there's no greater accolade. Don't get changed. What you're wearing is the uniform of hard work and the team will love you just the way you are.'

CHAPTER FIVE

THE TEAM KNOCKED off at five but Matt didn't. Matt owned the place. No one gave him a knock-off time. He and Nugget headed out round the paddocks, making sure all was well. Thankfully, the night was warm and still, so even the just-shorn sheep seemed settled. He returned to the homestead, checked the sheep in the pens for the morning and headed for the house.

Then he remembered the chooks; Donald hadn't fed them for a week now. He went round the back of the house and almost walked into Penny.

'All present and correct,' she told him. 'At least I think so. Fourteen girls, all safely roosted.'

'How did you know?'

'I saw you do it last night. I took a plate of leftovers down to Donald and saw they were still out. I don't know how you're coping with everything. You must be exhausted.'

'It's shearing time,' he told her simply. 'Every sheep farmer in the country feels like this. It only lasts two weeks.'

She eyed him sideways in the fading light. He waited for a comment but none came.

She'd changed again, into jeans and a windcheater. She looked extraordinarily young. Vulnerable.

Kind of like she needed protecting?

'Thank you for thinking of Donald.'

'He wouldn't come in with the shearers so I saved some for him. I think he was embarrassed but he took it.' She hesitated a moment but then decided to forge on. 'Matt…he told me he had to put Jindalee on the market but it broke his heart. And then you came. You renovated the cottage for him, even extending it so he could fit in everything he loved. And he can stay here for ever. I think that's lovely, Matt Fraser.'

'It's a two-way deal,' Matt growled, embarrassed. 'Don knows every inch of this land. I'm still learning from him. And I bet he appreciated the food. How you had the time to make those slices…'

'For arvo tea?' She grinned. 'I even have the jargon right. There'll be cakes tomorrow, now I'm more organized.'

'I'll pay you.'

'I don't need…'

'I'd have paid Pete. A lot. You'll get what he was contracted for.'

'You're giving me board and lodging.'

'And you're feeding a small army. I know it's a mere speck in the ocean compared to the money your family has, but I need to pay you.'

'Why?'

'So I can yell at you?' He grinned. 'I haven't yet but you should hear the language in the sheds.'

'Margie and Greta don't mind?'

'They use it themselves. As an official shearers' cook, you're entitled as well.'

'Thank you. I think.'

He chuckled and they walked back to the house together. The night seemed to close in on them.

The moon was rising in the east. An owl was starting its plaintive call in the gums above their heads.

She was so close…

'There's a plate of food in the warming oven,' she said prosaically and he gave himself a mental shake and tried to be prosaic back.

'There's no need. I could have cooked myself…'

'An egg?' She gave him a cheeky grin. 'After my lesson last night you might do better, but if you're hungry check what's in the oven first.'

'You're going to bed now?'

'If it's okay with you, I might sit on the veranda and soak up the night until I settle. It's been a crazy day and here's pretty nice,' she said diffidently.

'It is, isn't it?' He hesitated and then decided: *Why not?* 'Mind if I join you?'

'It's your house.'

'That's not what I asked.'

She stopped and looked up at him. Her gaze was suddenly serious. There was a long pause.

'No,' she said at last. 'I don't mind if you join me. I don't mind at all.'

She should go to bed. She shouldn't be sitting on the edge of the veranda listening to the owls— waiting for Matt.

Why did it seem dangerous?

It wasn't dangerous. He was her employer. Today had been a baptism of fire into the world of cooking for shearers and she needed downtime. He'd asked to join her—it was his veranda so how could she have said no?

She could change her mind even now and disappear.

So why wasn't she?

'Because I'm an idiot with men. The only guys I've ever dated have turned out to be focused on my family's money.' She said it out loud and Samson, curled up by her side, whined and looked up at her.

'But I do a great line in choosing dogs,' she told him, and tucked him onto her knee and fondled his ears. 'That's my forte. Dogs and cooking.'

He still looked worried—and, strangely, so was she. Because Matt Fraser was coming to join her on the veranda?

'He's my employer,' she told Samson. 'Nothing else. He could be a seventy-year-old grandpa with grandchildren at heel for all the difference it makes. I'm over men. Matt's my boss, and that's all.'

So why were warning signals flashing neon in her brain?

Leftovers? He stared at the plate incredulously. These were some leftovers!

The midday meal had been crazy. For the shearers it was a break, a time where they stopped and had a decent rest. They'd come in and seen Penny's food and basically fallen on it like ravenous wolves. Then they'd settled on the veranda to enjoy it.

Meanwhile, Matt had grabbed a couple of rolls and headed back to the shed. The shearers' break was his only chance to clear the place and get it ready for the next hard session.

Shearing was exhausting. He'd been supervising it since he was a teenager and he'd never become used to it. Even when Pete was here, the best shearers' cook in the district, Matt usually ended up kilos lighter by the end of the shear. He'd come in after dark and eat what he could find, which generally wasn't much. Shearers didn't leave much.

But Penny must have noticed, for in the warming drawer was a plate with all the best food from midday.

It hadn't been sitting in the oven all afternoon either. She must have guessed he'd come in at dark, or maybe she'd asked one of the men.

He poured himself a beer, grabbed his plate and headed out to the veranda. He settled himself on one of the big cane settees. Penny was in front of him, on the edge of the veranda, her legs swinging over the garden bed below.

'Thank you,' he said simply.

'You're welcome.'

Silence. It wasn't an uncomfortable silence though. Matt was concentrating on the truly excellent food and Penny seemed content just to sit and listen to the owl and swing her legs. She was idly petting her dog but Samson seemed deeply asleep.

Samson had spent the day investigating chooks, making friends with the farm dogs and checking out the myriad smells of the place. This afternoon he'd even attempted a bit of herding but some things were never going to work. Matt had plucked him from the mob, hosed him down and locked him in the kitchen with Penny.

There'd be worse places to be locked, Matt thought idly, and then thought *whoa*, Penny was his shearers' cook. It was appropriate to think of her only as that.

'So where did you learn to cook?' he asked as he finally, regretfully finished his last spoonful of pie.

'Not at my mother's knee,' she said and he thought about stopping there, not probing further. But there was something about the night, about this woman…

'I'd have guessed that,' he told her. 'The article I read… It doesn't suggest happy families.'

'You got it.'

'So…cooking?'

She sighed. 'My family's not exactly functional,' she told him. 'You read about Felicity? She's my half-sister. Her mother's an ex-supermodel, floating in and out of Felicity's life at whim. My mother was Dad's reaction to a messy divorce—and, I suspect, to his need for capital. Mum was an heiress, but she's a doormat and the marriage has been… troubled. To be honest, I don't think Dad even likes Mum any more but she won't leave him. And my sister… Even though Mum's been nothing but kind to Felicity, Felicity barely tolerates Mum, and she hates me. My life's been overlaid with my mother's mantras—avoid Felicity's venom and keep my father happy at all costs. So my childhood wasn't exactly happy. The kitchen staff were my friends.'

'So cooking became your career?'

'It wasn't my first choice,' she admitted. 'I wanted to be a palaeontologist. How cool would that have been?'

'A…what?'

'Studier of dinosaurs. But of course my father didn't see a future in it.'

'I wonder why not?'

'Don't you laugh,' she said sharply. 'That's what he did. I was the dumpy one, the one who hated my mother's hairdresser spending an hour giving me ringlets, the one who'd rather be climbing trees than sitting in the drawing room being admired by my parents' friends. And then, of course, I was expelled from school...'

'Expelled?' He'd been feeling sleepy, lulled by the night, the great food, the fatigue—and this woman's presence. Now his eyes widened. 'Why?'

'Quite easy in the end,' she told him. 'I don't understand why I didn't think of it earlier. I didn't mind being expelled in the least. It was boarding school—of course—the most elite girls' school my father could find. But I wasn't very...elite.'

She kicked her legs up and wiggled her bare toes in front of her and he could see how she might not be described as elite.

She wasn't elite. She was fascinating.

'I hated it,' she told him bluntly. 'I was there to be turned into a young lady. We had a whole afternoon every week of deportment, for heaven's sake. We learned to climb in and out of a car so no one can catch a sight of knickers.'

'Really?'

'It sounds funny,' she told him. 'It wasn't. I learned to wrangle a purse, a cocktail and an oyster at the same time, but it's a skill that's overrated.'

'I guess it could be.' She had him entranced. 'So...'

'So?'

'Expulsion? Explain.'

'Oh,' she said and grinned. 'That was our an-
nual ball. Very posh. We invited the local Very
Elite Boys' School. Deportment classes gave way
to dancing lessons and everyone had Very Expensive new frocks. And hairstyles. It was the culmi-
nation of the school year.'

'So...'

'So you might have noticed I'm little,' she told
him. 'And...well endowed?'

'I hadn't,' he told her and she choked.

'Liar. I'm a size D cup and it's the bane of my
life. But my mother bought me a frock and she was
so delighted by it I didn't have the heart to tell her
I hated it. It was crimson and it was low-cut, with
an underwire that pushed everything up.'

He had the vision now. He blinked. 'Wow.'

'My mother's willowy,' she said, with just a trace
of sympathy for a woman who'd never understood
her daughter's figure. 'It would have looked elegant
on Mum, but on me? It just made me look like a
tart, and it got attention.' She paused for breath.
'Rodney Gareth was a horrid little toad, but sadly
he was also the son of Malcolm Gareth QC, who's a
horrid big toad. Rodney asked me to dance. He held
me so tight my boobs were crushed hard against
him. He swaggered all over the dance floor with
me and I could feel his...excitement. I could hear
the other girls laughing. And then...'

She fell silent for a moment and he thought she was going to stop. 'And then?' It'd kill him if he didn't get any further, he thought, but she relented.

'We all had these dinky little dance programmes, with pencils attached,' she said. 'And, before I could stop him, he pulled mine from my wrist and held it up, pretending to check for my next free dance. And then he deliberately dropped the pencil down my cleavage.'

'Uh oh,' he said.

'Uh oh is right,' she said bitterly. 'I was standing in the middle of the dance floor and suddenly he shoved his whole hand down there. And people started laughing...'

'Oh, Penny.'

'So I kneed him right where it hurt most,' she said. 'I used every bit of power I had. I still remember his scream. It was one of the more satisfying moments of my life but of course it didn't last. I felt sick and cheap and stained. I walked out of the ball, back to my dorm, ripped my stupid dress off and called a cab to take me home. And don't you dare laugh.'

'I never would.' He hesitated. 'Penny... Did your parents laugh?'

'They were appalled. Mum was horrified. She could see how upset I was. But Dad? The first thing he did was ring Rodney's parents to find out if he was okay. His father told Dad they weren't sure if I'd interfered with the Gareth family escutcheon. He said they were taking him to hospital to check—I hadn't, by the way—and they intended to sue. Then the headmistress rang and said I wasn't welcome back at the school. Dad was furious and Mum's never had the nerve to stand up to him.'

'So what happened?'

'So I was packed off to Switzerland to a finishing school. That pretty much knocked any idea of being a palaeontologist on the head but, on the other hand, they ran cooking classes because that was supposed to be seemly, and if I wanted to do five cooking classes a week that was okay by them. So we had Monsieur Fromichade who I promptly fell in love with, even though I was sixteen and he was sixty. We still exchange recipes.'

'So happy ever after?'

She grimaced. 'It worked for a while. I took every cooking course I could and that was okay. Dad approved of what he told his friends were my three star Michelin intentions. Finally I took a job as an apprentice in a London café. It was simple food, nothing epicure about it. But I loved it.'

She paused, seemingly reluctant to expose any more of her family's dirty linen, but then she shrugged and continued. 'But then things fell apart at home.' She sighed. 'My sister had been overseas for years. There were rumours circulating about her behaviour on the Riviera and somehow Dad made

it all Mum's fault. He's always favoured Felicity
and he blamed Mum for her leaving home. Then
Grandma died and Mum…got sick. Depression.
She started phoning every day, weeping, begging
me to come home. Finally I caved. I came home
and Mum was in such a state I was frightened. I
even agreed to what my Dad wanted, for me to be
a company PR assistant. I thought I'd do it for a
while, just until Mum recovered.'

She shrugged again. 'And it worked for a while.
With me around to stand up for her, Dad stopped
being such a bully. That took the pressure off Mum
and things looked better. For Mum, though, not for
me. And then Brett decided to court me.'

'Brett?' He shouldn't ask but how could he help
it?

'It seems every guy I've ever dated has turned
out to be fascinated by my parents' money,' she
said bluntly. 'So I should have known. But maybe
I was vulnerable, too. Brett's yet another toad, but
I was too dumb and, to be honest, I was too unhappy and caught up in family drama to see it. I
hadn't realized until I got home how close to the
edge Mum was, and I was scared. I was trying
every way I knew to make her feel good. Brett's
a financial guru, smart, savvy and he knows how
to pander to Dad. He's also good-looking and oh,
so charming. In those awful months Brett helped.
He honestly did. You have no idea how charming

he was. He made me feel…special, and when he asked me to marry him I was dumb enough to say yes.'

'So celebrations all round?'

'You think?' she said bitterly. 'You know, the moment I said yes I had my doubts but I'm my mother's daughter. Dad was happy. Mum was well. For a while it was happy families all round. But then Felicity returned and Brett realized Felicity was Dad's absolute favourite and he could be part of our family and not have to sacrifice himself with the dumpy one.'

'Humiliation piled on humiliation,' he said softly and she cast him a glance that was almost scared.

'Yeah. I was paying too big a price to keep people happy and I've realized it. I'm over it.'

'I'm sure you're not.'

And she managed a smile. 'Maybe not quite, but I will be after a year's cooking at Malley's.'

'You can't go there.'

'When the water goes down, of course I can.'

'You'll hate it. The last time Malley set a mouse trap… Well, I've never seen one. What I have seen are dead mice.'

'Ugh!'

'Everywhere. He baits them and doesn't bother to clean.

'I can clean,' she said in a small voice.

'I bet you can but you shouldn't have to. Don't

Mummy and Daddy supply you with enough money to be fancy-free?'

'That's offensive.'

'True.'

'Okay,' she conceded. 'Dad holds the purse strings but a legacy from Grandma left me basically independent. Not rich, but okay. Eventually I might set up a catering company in Adelaide or in Brisbane, but for now I need time to get my head together. I need to be as far from Sydney as possible.'

'Which is why you headed into the outback in *that* car?'

Now she grinned. 'Isn't it fun? Dad probably wants it back, though. He gave it to me when Brett and I got engaged. With a huge pink ribbon on it. I was momentarily the golden girl.'

'Shall we take it back to the creek and launch it? Let it float ceremoniously a few hundred miles to the ocean?'

She stared. 'Pardon?'

'We could take pictures of it floating out of sight and send them to your father. Very symbolic.'

She choked. 'Dad'd have a stroke. To say he's careful is an understatement.'

'But not careful of his daughter,' Matt said, his voice softening.

'Don't.'

'Don't what?'

'Get sympathetic. I'm fine as long as no one minds.'

'So no one minds?'

'No,' she said fiercely. 'No one at all. That last awful dinner, when Brett and Felicity walked in hand in hand, Mr and Mrs Smug…I was too gobsmacked to yell and Mum didn't have the strength to stand up for me. But I guess that was my line in the sand. I can't help Mum and I won't keep trying to please my father. And in a way it's liberating. I've walked away. I'm free.'

Then she paused. The night stilled and he thought of what he should say next.

But she got there before him.

'So what about you?' she asked.

He'd finished his beer. He was tired beyond belief. He should pick up his dishes and head via the kitchen to bed.

'What do you mean, what about me?'

'Who minds?' she asked. 'That's what you asked me. Who cares, Matt Fraser? You live here by yourself. No girlfriend? Boyfriend? Whatever?'

'I have a…' he said slowly, and then he paused. He didn't want to talk about Lily.

But this woman had just opened herself to him. She might say she was free, she was over being hurt, but he knew vulnerable when he saw it.

She'd trusted him with her story. How mean would it be not to give the same to her?

He tried again. 'I have a daughter,' he told her. 'Lily's thirteen years old and lives in the States with my ex-wife.'

She'd been gazing out over the farmland but now she swivelled to stare at him. He hadn't turned the porch lights on, but the moonlight and the light filtering from inside the windows was enough for her to see.

Not that he wanted her to see. He wanted his face to be impassive.

Which was pretty much how he wanted to be when he thought of Lily.

'Thirteen! You must have been a baby when she was born,' she stammered and he thought: *Yep, that just about summed it up.*

'I was twenty-four.'

'Wow.' She was still staring. 'So your wife took Lily back to the States. Isn't that hard to do? I mean…did you consent?'

'Darrilyn met an investment banker, coming to investigate…a project I was working on. He was rich, he lived in New York, she was fascinated and he offered her a more exciting life than the one she had with me. She was also four months pregnant. When you leave Australia with your child, the child needs the permission of both parents. When you're pregnant no one asks.'

'Oh, Matt…'

'It's okay,' he said, even though it wasn't. 'I have the resources to see her a couple of times a year.'

'Does she look like you?'

And, for some reason, that shook him.

The guys on the farm knew he had a daughter—that was the reason he took off twice a year—but that was as far as it went. When had he ever talked about his daughter? Never.

'I guess she does,' he said slowly. 'She has my black hair. My brown eyes. There's no denying parentage, if that's what you mean.'

'I guess. I didn't mean anything,' she whispered. 'I'm just thinking how hard it would be to leave her there.' She gave herself a shake, a small physical act that said she was moving on from something that was clearly none of her business. But it seemed she did have more questions, just not about Lily.

'So you,' she said. 'I've told you all about my appalling family. Your mum and dad?'

'Just mum.' Why was he telling her this? He should excuse himself and go to bed. But he couldn't. She was like a puppy, he thought, impossible to kick.

Or was there more? The need to talk? He never talked but he did now.

'This farm,' she was saying. 'I assumed you'd inherited it.'

'Sort of.'

'So rich mum, hey?'

'The opposite.' He hated talking about it but he forced himself to go on. 'Mum had me when she was eighteen and she had no support. I was a latch-key kid from early on, but we coped.' He didn't say how they'd coped. What use describing a childhood where he'd been needed to cope with his mother's emotional messes?

'Give me a hug, sweetheart. Sorry, I can't stop crying. Can you go out and buy pies for tea? Can you go down to the welfare and say Mummy's not well, we need money for food? But say I've just got the flu... I don't want them sticking their noses in here...'

He shook himself, shoving back memories that needed to be buried. Penny was waiting for him to go on.

'When I was twelve Mum took a housekeeping job about five hundred miles inland from Perth,' he told her. 'Sam Harriday was an eighty-year-old bachelor. He'd worked his parents' farm on his own for years and was finally admitting he needed help. So off we went, to somewhere Mum hoped we'd be safe.'

'Safe?'

'Sorry.' He caught himself, but now he'd said it he had to explain. A bit. 'There were parts of Mum's life that weren't safe.'

She was silent at that, and he thought she'd

probe. He didn't want her to but he'd asked for it. But when she spoke again she'd moved on. Maybe she'd sensed his need for barriers. 'Good for your mum,' she told him. 'But so far inland… You were twelve? How did you go to school?'

'School of the Air.' He shrugged and smiled at the memory of his not very scholastic self. 'Not that I studied much. I took one look at the farm and loved it. And Sam…' He hesitated. 'Well, Sam was a mate. He could see how hungry I was to learn and he taught me.'

'But—' she frowned, obviously trying to figure the whole story '—this isn't his farm?'

'It's not,' he told her. 'Cutting a long story short, when I was fifteen Mum fell for a biker who got lost and asked for a bed. She followed him to the city but Sam offered to let me stay. So I did. I kept up with School of the Air until I was seventeen but by then I was helping him with everything. And I loved it. I loved him. He died when I was twenty-two and he left me everything.' He shrugged. 'An inheritance seems great until you realize what comes with it. The death of someone you love.'

'I'm sorry…'

'It's a while back now and it was his time,' he said, but he paused, allowing a moment for the memories of the old man he'd loved. Allowing himself to remember again the pain that happened when he'd been needed so much, and suddenly there was no one.

'So the farm was mine,' he managed, shaking off memories of that time of grief. It was rough country, a farm you had to sweat to make a living from, but it did have one thing going for it that I hadn't realized. It was sitting on a whole lot of bauxite. That's the stuff used to make aluminium. Apparently geologists had approached Sam over the years but he'd always seen them off. After he died one of them got in touch with me. We tested and the rest is history.'

'You own a bauxite mine?' she said incredulously and he laughed.

'I own a great sheep property. This one. I own a couple more properties down river—economies of scale make it worthwhile—but this place is my love. I also own a decent share of a bauxite mine. That was what got me into trouble, though. It's why Darrilyn married me, though I was too dumb to see it. But I'm well over it. My current plan is to make this the best sheep station in the state, if not the country, and the fact that I seem to have hauled the best shearers' cook I can imagine out of the creek is a bonus.'

He smiled and rose, shaking off the ghosts that seemed to have descended. 'Enough. If I don't go to bed now I'll fall asleep on top of a pile of fleece tomorrow. Goodnight, Penny.'

She stood up too, but she was still frowning. 'The mine,' she said. 'Bauxite… Sam Harriday… It's not Harriday Holdings?'

'That's the one.'

'Oh, my,' she gasped. 'Matt, my father tried to invest in that mine. He couldn't afford to.'

'The shares are tightly held.'

'By you?'

'Mostly.'

She stood back from him and she was suddenly glaring. 'That must make you a squillionaire.'

'I told you I'd pay you. Now you know I can afford to. And I doubt I'm a squillionaire.' He shrugged. 'I don't even know what one is. And, by the way, I'd appreciate it if you didn't broadcast it. The locals don't know and I have no idea why I told you.'

'Because it's our night for secrets?' She hesitated and then reached out to touch his hand. 'Matt?'

He looked down at her hand on his. It looked wrong, he thought. This was a gesture of comfort and he didn't need comfort. Or maybe she intended to ask a question that needed it.

'Yes?' That was brusque. He tried again and got it better. 'Yes?'

'Where's your mother now?'

How had she guessed? he thought incredulously. How had she seen straight through his story to the one thing that hurt the most?

'Dead.'

'I'm sorry. But something tells me…'

'Don't!'

She hesitated and then her hand came up and touched his cheek, a feather-touch, a fleeting gesture of warmth.

'I won't ask but I'm sorry,' she whispered. 'And I'm even more sorry because…you might be a squillionaire, but something tells me that all the whinging I've just done doesn't come close to the pain you're hiding. Thank you for rescuing me yesterday, Matt Fraser. I just wish I could rescue you right back.'

CHAPTER SIX

IF EVER THERE was a cure for humiliation piled on humiliation, it was ten days of cooking for shearers. Ten days of pure hard work.

'We've only two more mobs left,' Matt told her with satisfaction. 'That's four days shearing and we're done. We've had the best weather. The best food. The best shear I've ever organised. You're our good luck charm, Penny Hindmarsh-Firth. I've a good mind to keep you.'

Matt hadn't stopped for ten days, Penny thought. He'd worked until after midnight almost every night. He said he went to bed but she saw his light at the far end of the veranda.

She had his situation pretty much summed up by now. Five sheep properties. A bauxite mine worth heaven only knew how much. Responsibilities everywhere.

The drapes in his bedroom were often pulled back. She could see his shadow against the light, sitting at his desk, working into the night.

He had a massive desk in his study. He wasn't using that.

Because she was here? She knew it was, but he wasn't avoiding her.

They'd fallen into a routine. Matt left the house

before dawn, she saw him only briefly at meals but at dusk she sat on the veranda and talked to the dogs and he'd finally fetch his plate of leftovers from the warming drawer and come out to join her.

He was always dead tired. She could hear it in his voice, in the slump of his shoulders. Sometimes he seemed almost too tired to talk and she respected that, but still he seemed to soak up her company. And for herself? She liked him being here too, and she didn't need to talk. She was content to sit and watch the moon rise over the horizon, to breathe in the night air and let go of her fast-paced day.

And it was fast-paced. She'd set herself a personal challenge. Each day's cooking had to be at least as good as the days' before. It was worth it. 'Great tucker,' a shearer growled as he headed back to work. Or, 'Strewth, Pen, that sponge's almost as good as my gran used to make.'

And Matt had nothing but praise. 'I'd have pulled a rhinoceros out of the creek to get cooking like this,' he'd told her after the first couple of days and she had no idea why that throwaway line had the capacity to make her feel as if her insides were glowing.

The way he ate her food at night was compliment enough. He was always past exhaustion but he sat and savoured her food as if every mouthful was gold. He was enjoying his dinner now, as she sat and watched the moon rise.

She thought about the way he'd smiled at her when she'd handed him his plate. Somehow he didn't feel like an employer. She wasn't sure what he felt like, but...

'Malley doesn't know what he's getting.' Matt's low growl from where he sat behind her made her jump. She'd been dreaming. Of a smile?

Idiot!

She didn't answer. There was nothing to say to such a compliment. There was no reason his comment should have her off balance.

Though, actually, there was.

There were four more days of shearing to go. The floodwaters were slowly going down. She could probably leave now, though it'd still be a risk. And Matt still needed her.

But in four days...

'You are still going to Malley's?' Matt asked and she tried to think of a way to say it, and couldn't.

But he guessed. Maybe her silence was answer enough. 'You've changed your mind?' Matt put his empty plate aside and came across to where she sat on the edge of the veranda. He slipped down beside her and the night seemed to close in around them, a warm and intimate space that held only them.

What was she thinking? *Intimate?* He was her boss!

He was a man and she didn't trust herself with men. Didn't they always want something? Something other than her? Even Matt. He needed her to cook. She was useful, nothing else.

So stop thinking of something else.

'Malley changed my mind,' she managed, and was disconcerted at the way her voice worked. Or didn't work. Why were emotions suddenly crowding in on her?

And it wasn't just how close Matt was sitting beside her, she thought. It was more. In four days she wouldn't be needed. Again.

Wasn't that what she wanted?

Oh, for heaven's sake, get over it, she told herself and swung her feet in an attempt at defiance.

As if sensing his mistress needed a bit of support, Samson edged sideways and crept up onto her knee. He was filthy but she didn't mind. Penny had given up on the bathing. Samson was now a farm dog.

If her mother could see her now she'd have kittens, Penny thought. She was filthy too, covered in the flour she'd used to prepare the bread dough for the morning. She was cradling a stinking poodle.

But Matt was sitting by her side and she thought, *I don't care. Mum has Felicity if she wants a beautiful daughter. I'm happy here.*

It was a strange thought—a liberating thought.

She tried to think of Brett. Or Felicity. Of the two of them hand in hand telling her they'd betrayed her.

They can have each other, she thought, and it was the first time she'd felt no bitterness.

Ten days of shearing had changed things. Ten days of sitting outside every night with Matt? But there were only four days to go.

'You going to tell me about Malley?' Matt asked. He'd given her time. He'd sensed there were things she was coming to terms with, but now he was asking again.

What had she told him? *Malley changed my mind.*

Yeah, he had, and she'd been upset and she should still be upset. But how hard was it to be angry when she was sitting with this man whose empathy twisted something inside her that she hadn't known existed.

'I phoned Malley the night I got here,' she admitted. 'He told me I was a…well, I won't say what he said but the gist of it was that I was a fool for taking the route I did and he was an idiot himself for thinking a citified b…a citified woman could do the job. He said he'd find someone else. He called me a whole lot of words I'd never heard of. I guess I was pretty upset so when he rang back and expected me to drop everything…'

And then she stopped. She hadn't meant to say

any more. What was it about this man that messed with her head? That messed with the plan of action she knew was sensible?

'Drop everything?' he said slowly, and she thought *uh oh*. She went to get up but he put his hand on her arm and held her still. 'You mean abandon this place?' He was frowning. 'Is that what he meant?'

'He rang me back two days after I got here,' she admitted. 'But it's okay. I used a few of his words back at him. Not...not the worst ones. But maybe the ones about being an idiot for ever thinking I'd take the job.'

'But why did he ring?'

This was sort of embarrassing. She'd been dumb to say anything at all but Matt was watching her. He was frowning, obviously thinking through the words she'd let slip. She had no choice but to be honest.

'He ended up almost as trapped as we are, so finding another cook wasn't an option,' she told him. 'And it's costing him. Malley's hotel is the base for scores of stranded tourists. He has supplies but no one to cook. He's losing a fortune.'

'So?' Matt said slowly.

'So he knows one of the chopper pilots who's doing feed drops up north. I gather for two days he fumed at how useless I was and then he realized he didn't have a choice. So he bribed the chopper pilot to come and get me.'

There was a loaded silence.

'So why didn't you go?'

'You told me he had mice.'

'And you told me you could clean.'

'So I could,' she said with sudden asperity. 'But I didn't see why I should clean for someone with such a foul mouth. The tourists can cook for themselves if they need to. Why should I go?'

'But you came all the way here to take a permanent, full-time job.'

'I did.'

'And shearing finishes in four days.' He frowned. 'Why didn't you accept? I don't understand.'

And she didn't, either. Not totally. It had been a decision of the heart, not the head, but she wasn't about to tell him that.

She reverted to being practical. 'The chopper pilot was supposed to be dropping food to stranded livestock, so what was he about, agreeing to pick me up? How could I live with myself knowing cows were hungry because of me? Besides, they couldn't fit my car into the chopper.'

'You were the one who suggested leaving your car here until after the floods.'

Drat, why did he have to have such a good memory?

'So why?' he asked again, more gently, and suddenly there seemed nothing left but the truth.

'You needed me,' she told him. 'And...'

'And?'

Her chin tilted. This was something her family never got. Her friends never got. She'd been mocked for this before but she might as well say it. 'I was having fun.'

'Fun?' He stared at her in amazement. 'You've worked harder than any shearer. You've planned, you've cooked, you've cleaned. You've gone to bed as exhausted as me every night and you've got up every morning and started all over again. You call that fun?'

'Yes.' She said it firmly. It was a stand she'd defended for years and she wasn't letting it go now. Cooking was her love, and cooking for people who appreciated it was heaven. 'But you needn't sound so amazed. Tell me why you're here. You own a bauxite mine, one of the richest in the country. You surely don't need to farm. You're working yourself into the ground too. For what?'

'Fun?' he said and she smiled.

'Gotcha.'

'Okay.' He sighed. 'I get it, though I'm imagining the work at Malley's would have been just as hard. So where do you go from here? You knocked back a permanent job to help me.'

'I knocked back a permanent job because I

wanted this one. And, even without the mice, Malley sounds mean.'

'The man's an imbecile,' Matt said. 'To badmouth a cook of your standard? He obviously has the brains of a newt. To lose you…'

And then he paused.

The atmosphere changed. That thing inside her twisted again. To have someone defend her…value her…

It's the cooking, she told herself. She was never valued for herself.

But suddenly his hand was covering hers, big and rough and warm. 'Thank you,' he told her and it sounded as if it came from the heart. 'Thank you indeed—and I think your wages just went up.'

Fun.

He thought of the massive amount of work she'd put in over the last ten days. He thought of the drudgery of planning, chopping, peeling, cooking and cleaning. He thought of the mounds of washing-up. How had he ever thought he could handle it himself? In the end he'd hardly had time to help her cart food across to the shed, but she hadn't complained once.

She was a pink princess, the daughter of one of the wealthiest families in Australia, yet she'd worked as hard as any shearer.

And in four days? Shearing would be over. The

water was already dropping in the creeks. Cooking at Malley's was obviously out of the question. Penny's long-term plan to set up a catering company would take months. Meanwhile, what would she do?

She'd come a long way to be here, and she'd come for a reason. She'd exposed her pain to him. She'd exposed the hurt her family had heaped on her. She was here to escape humiliation—and now, because she'd decided to help him she had little choice but to head back and face that humiliation again. Even if she went to another city the media would find her. He had no doubt the media frenzy during her sister's wedding would be appalling.

'Stay for a bit,' he found himself saying. Until the words were out of his mouth he didn't know he'd intended to say them, but the words were said. He'd asked the pink princess to stay.

There was a moment's silence. Actually, it was more than a moment. It stretched on.

She was considering it from all angles, he thought, and suddenly he wondered if she was as aware as he was of the tension between them.

Tension? It was the wrong word but he didn't have one to replace it. It was simply the way she made him feel.

She was little and blonde and cute. She played Abba on her sound system while she worked and she sang along. This morning he'd come in to help her cart food over to the shed and found her spinning to *Dancing Queen* while balancing a tray of blueberry muffins. She'd had flour on her nose, her curls had escaped the piece of pink ribbon she'd used to tie them back and Samson was barking at her feet with enthusiasm.

He'd stopped at the door and watched, giving himself a moment before she realized he was there. He'd watched and listened and he'd felt…

It didn't matter how he'd felt. He didn't *do* women. His mother and then Darrilyn had taught him everything he needed to know about the pain of relationships and he wasn't going there again. Especially with an indulged society princess.

The label wasn't fair, he told himself, and he knew it was the truth. Penny had proved she was so much more. But past pain had built armour he had no desire to shed, and right now he felt his armour had to be reinforced. Yet here he was asking her to stay.

'Why would I stay?' Penny asked cautiously and he tried to think of an answer that was sensible.

'I… This place…I was thinking maybe I could open it up a bit. Get rid of a few dustcovers. There's a possibility my daughter might come and visit.' That was the truth, though he wasn't sure when. 'I wouldn't mind if it looked a bit more like a home when she came. Maybe you could help. I'd pay.'

'I don't need…'

'I know you don't need to be paid,' he said. 'But I pay for services rendered. The shearers will move on, but I'd need you for another two weeks in total—a few days' slack then getting the house in order. Of course—' he grinned suddenly '—cooking would be in there as well. Donald and Ron and Harv would kill me if I didn't say that. They've been in heaven for the last ten days.'

And then he paused and tried to think about why he shouldn't say what came next. There were reasons but they weren't strong enough to stop him. 'And so have I,' he added.

Heaven...

That was pretty much what she was feeling.

She was breathing in the scents from the garden, watching the moon rise over the distant hills, listening to the odd bleat of a sheep in the shearing pens and the sound of a bird in the gums at the garden's edge.

'What's the bird?' she asked. It was an inconsequential question, a question to give her space and time to think through what he was proposing. There was a part of her that said what he was suggesting was unwise, but she couldn't figure out why.

Or maybe she knew why; she just didn't want to admit it. The way he made her feel… The way his smile made her heart twist…

'It's a boobook owl,' Matt said, quietly now, as

if there was no big question between them. 'It's a little brown owl, nocturnal. He and his mate are the reason we don't have mice and places like Malley's do. Malley's stupid enough to have cleared the trees around the hotel and he's probably even stupid enough to shoot them. They're great birds. Listen to their call. *Boobook*. Or sometimes people call them mopokes for the same reason. So there's a question for you. Do you side with mopoke or boobook?'

It was an ideal question. It gave her time to sit and listen, to settle.

'Mopoke,' she said at last. 'Definitely mopoke.'

'I'm a boobook man myself. Want to see?'

'You need to go to bed.'

'So do you, but life's too short to miss a boobook.'

'A mopoke.'

He grinned. 'That's insubordination,' he told her. 'I believe I've just offered you a job for the next two weeks. Therefore I demand you accept your boss's edict that it's a boobook.'

'I haven't agreed to take the job yet.'

'So you haven't,' he said equitably. 'But you are still employed for four more days. So it's boobook tonight.' He pushed himself to his feet and held out his hand to help her up. 'Come and see.'

She looked at his offered hand and thought...*I shouldn't.*

And then she thought: *Why not?* There were all sorts of reasons, but Matt was smiling down at her and his hand was just there.

She shouldn't take it—but she did.

What was he doing?

He was more than tired. By this stage in shearing he was operating on autopilot. He'd averaged about five hours of sleep a night for the past ten days and, apart from the tiny window of time on the veranda at night, every minute he was awake was crammed with imperatives. Most of those imperatives involved tough manual labour but he also had to be fine-tuned to the atmosphere in the shed. One flare-up could mess with a whole shear. Angry shearers usually meant sloppy shearing and the flock suffered.

So far the tension had been minimal. The shearers had worked through each run looking forward to Penny's next meal, bantering about the last. This shear was amazing and it was pretty much thanks to the woman beside him. So surely he could take a few minutes to show her a boobook?

Besides, he wanted to.

He had a torch in his pocket. It was strong but it was small, casting a narrow band of light in front of them as they walked. They needed to go into the stand of gums behind the house. The ground was thick with leaf litter and fallen twigs so it was natural—even essential—that he keep hold of her hand. After all, she was a vital cog in his business empire. He needed to take care of her.

Even though it made him feel… How did he feel?

Good. That was too small a word but his mind wasn't prepared to think of another. Her fingers were laced in his and her hand was half his size. His fingers were calloused and rough, too rough to be holding something as warm and…trusting?

That was what it felt like but that was dumb. He'd figured enough of Penny by now to know that she could look after herself. One move that she didn't like would have her screeching the farm down, and an inkling of Penny in peril would have the entire shearing team out in force.

He grinned at the thought and Penny must have heard his smile. 'What's the joke?'

'I just thought…if I tried a bit of seduction you'd have the team out here ready to defend you. Shears at the ready. Ron was watching you go back to the house yesterday and said you had a nice rear end. Margie told him where he could put his sexist comments and suddenly we had the whole shearing shed coming down on Ron like a ton of bricks. The poor guy had to bury himself packing fleeces into the wool press for the rest of the afternoon. You have an army at your disposal, Penelope Hindmarsh-Firth.'

'Excellent,' she said and smiled and was it his

imagination or did her hold on his hand tighten a little? She paused for a moment as if she was thinking of something important—or trying to find the courage to say something—and finally out it came.

'Do you think I have a nice…rear end?'

Whoa. 'You have a very nice rear end,' he admitted. Who could argue with the truth?

'Thank you,' she told him. 'Yours isn't so bad either.'

That set him back. A woman telling him he had a good butt?

'But don't let it go to your head,' she told him. 'And I'll try and swallow my conceit too. Where did you say these owls are?'

The calls had ceased. That was because they were standing right under the trees the birds were nesting in.

It took him a moment to collect himself and direct his torchlight up. She disconcerted him. She was so close. She still smelled faintly yeasty, from the bread she'd set to rise. From something citrusy in her hair. From…being Penny?

What was he here for? He was looking for owls. *Right.*

'There…' Penny breathed—she'd caught sight of the first bird before he had. Even though he was holding the torch. *Good one, Fraser*, he told himself. *Get a grip.*

'The other will be close,' he managed.

'The other?'

'This is a nesting pair. They've been using the same nest for years, very successfully. Their young populate half this valley. Look, there's the female. She's a bit bigger than the male. They're feeling a bit threatened now. See, they're sitting bolt upright, but they've seen me so often I can't imagine they think of me as a threat.'

He was concentrating on the birds rather than Penny.

'Would the shearing team leap to their defence too?' she asked mildly and he smiled.

'They might. No one likes their quarters over-run by mice. These guys do us a favour. But I don't think they'd come quite as fast as if you needed help. You've—deservedly—made some pretty fierce friends.'

'Matt?'

'Mmm?'

'Stop it with the compliments. They don't mean anything and I don't want them.'

And the way she said it made him pause. It made him stop thinking of how she smelled and, instead, think about where she'd come from.

He got it, he thought. She'd just been through one messy relationship. He didn't know this Brett guy who'd been such a toe-rag but he could imagine. Somehow, he had a pretty clear idea of her family dynamics by now. In some ways Penny was tough but in others…she was exposed, he thought, and Brett must have sensed that weakness. If he'd said great things to her she would have believed them. She'd believed them all the way to a calamitous engagement.

So now she thought compliments were a means of manipulation and he could understand why. He had to shut up. Except suddenly he couldn't.

'Right,' he told her. 'No more compliments. But there are a few truths—not compliments, truths, that I'm not taking back. Firstly, your cooking is awesome and I'm incredibly grateful. Second, I'd agree with Ron—you do have a nice rear end, even though it's an entirely inappropriate comment for a boss to make about his employee. And finally there's one more thing which I need to say and it'll make you blush because it's a ripper.'

'A ripper?' she said faintly. 'A ripper of a compliment?'

'Not a compliment,' he told her, throwing caution to the wind. He took her other hand and tugged so she was facing him. 'Just the truth. Penelope Hindmarsh-Firth, you smell of fresh baked bread and yeast and the aroma of a day spent in the kitchen, my kitchen, and if you think me telling you that you have a nice backside is an empty compliment then the world's upside down. This is a gorgeous night and I'm holding the hands of a woman who's saved my butt. She has a beau-

tiful backside, not to mention the rest of her—
and she smells and looks beautiful. Messy but
beautiful. No more compliments, Penny. Just the
truth. So...'

He paused then and took a deep breath and
fought for the strength to say what had to be said.
Because it was unwise and shouldn't be said at all
but how could he not?

'So?' she whispered and somehow he found himself answering. Still telling it like it was.

'So we need to go in now because if we stay out
here one moment longer I'll be forced to kiss you.'

And there it was, out in the open. This thing...

'And you don't want to?' It was a whisper, so
low he thought he'd misheard. But he hadn't. Her
whisper seemed to echo. Even the owls above their
head seemed to pause to listen.

This was such a bad idea. This woman was his
employee. She was trapped here for the next four
days, or longer if she took him up on his offer to
extend.

What was he doing? Standing in the dark, talking of kissing a woman? Did he want to?

'I do want to,' he said because there was nothing else to say.

'Then what's stopping you?'

'Penny...'

'Just shut up, Matt Fraser, and kiss me.'

And what could he say to that?

The night held its breath and Matt Fraser took Penny Hindmarsh-Firth into his arms and he kissed her.

Wow.
   Um...
   Wow?
This was wrong on so many levels. Firstly, she should still be in mourning for her broken engagement and the betrayal that went with it.

Second, this man was her boss.

Third, she was alone out here, under the gums and the starlight with a man she'd met less than two weeks ago.

The owls above their heads had decided they no longer needed to be wary and were swooping off, dark shadows against the moonlight as they continued their night's hunt.

Under her feet was a carpet of leaf litter that gave off the scent of eucalypts when she moved. But how could she move?

Matt was tugging her close. Her face was tilting up to his and his mouth met hers.

Matt hadn't shaved for a couple of days—when would he find time? His clothes were rough, heavy moleskin pants and a thick shirt open at the throat, sleeves rolled back to reveal arms of sheer brawn. His hands were scarred and weathered.

He smelled of the shearing shed. He'd washed

and changed before he'd come out to the veranda but the lanolin from the fleeces seemed to have seeped into his pores. He smelled and felt what he was. He owned this land but he stood beside his men. He did the hard yards with them.

He was a man of steel.

He kissed her as if this was the first time for both of them. As if he had all the time in the world. As if he wasn't sure what it was he'd be tasting but he wasn't about to rush it.

His hands moved to her hips but he didn't tug her into him, or if he did it wasn't hard, and maybe the fact that she was melting against him was an act of her own volition. She could back away at any time.

But oh, the feel of him. The sensation of his lips brushing hers. For now it was just brushing, almost a feather-touch, but it was the most sensual thing she'd ever felt. His hands on the small of her back… The feel of his rough hair as she tentatively lifted her hand and let herself rake it…

Oh, Matt.

Oh, wow.

But he wasn't pressing. He wasn't pushing and suddenly she saw it from his point of view.

She was in his terrain, and she was all by herself. He was a man of honour. He was kissing her on terms that said the control was hers. She could pull back.

And with that thought came the most logical next thought.

If she was in control then bring it on. How could she not? This man was gorgeous. The night was gorgeous. She was a twenty-seven-year-old woman out under the stars with a man to die for.

And then, quite deliberately, she let her thoughts dissolve. She raised her hands to his hair so she had his head and she tugged him closer. She stood on tiptoe to get closer still.

She opened her lips and she welcomed him in.

Penny was melting under his hands and there wasn't a thing he could do about it.

How could he want to do anything about it?

She'd stood on tiptoe and surrendered her mouth to him. Her hands claimed him. Her body said she wanted this kiss as much or more than he did, and he'd better get on with it.

And so he did, and the sensation was enough to do his head in. The warmth, the heat, the fire… The night was dissolving in a mist of desire where nothing existed except this woman in his arms. This woman kissing him as fiercely as he kissed her. This woman whose body language said she wanted him as much as he wanted her.

A moment in time that was indescribable. Inevitable. World-changing?

The moment stretched on, a man and a woman in the moonlight, almost motionless, welded together by the heat from this kiss. From this need.

From this recognition that something was changing for both of them?

And with that thought…*trouble.*

It was as if his past had suddenly flown back, a cold chill of memory. Of love given and not returned. Of faith and trust blasted. Of the emptiness of loss. The grief…

He felt it almost as a physical jolt and, as if she'd felt it, she was suddenly tugging back. Maybe she'd had the same jolt of uncertainty, the same frisson that their worlds were both under threat by some new order.

And it almost killed him, but he let her go.

'W…wow,' she breathed and he thought: *Good description.* He couldn't think of a better word himself.

'You kiss good,' she managed. She looked dazed. A curl had escaped her ponytail and was coiling down across her eyes. He couldn't help himself— he lifted it and pushed it back.

But he didn't take her back into his arms.

'You're not so bad yourself,' he ventured, but the ghosts had been right to tug him back. He had no intention of getting involved with any woman. He would not face that kind of grief again.

But this wasn't any woman. This was Penny.

'We…we should be careful.' She couldn't quite disguise the quaver in her voice. 'If we go any further we'll shock the owls.'

'Probably not wise,' he managed.

'None of this is wise,' she whispered. 'But I'm not sure I care.'

It was up to him. And somehow he made the call. Somehow the ghosts prevailed.

'I need to be up before dawn,' he told her.

There was a long silence. Then, 'Of course you do.' There was still a tremble in her voice but she was fighting to get it under control.

Somehow he stayed silent. Somehow he managed not to gather her into his arms and take this to its inevitable conclusion.

It almost killed him.

But she had herself under control now. He could see her gathering herself together. This was a woman used to being rebuffed, he thought, and somehow that made it worse. But the ghosts were all around him, echoes of lessons long learned.

He didn't move.

'Then goodnight, Matt,' she whispered at last, and she reached out and touched his face in the most fleeting of farewell caresses. 'Sleep well. Sleep happy and sensible.'

And she turned and, without a torch, not even noticing the rough ground, she practically ran back to the relative sanctuary of the house.

It was done.

Sense had prevailed.

CHAPTER SEVEN

THEY WORKED SOLIDLY for the next four days. The timetable remained the same. They hardly saw each other during the day but at night Matt continued bringing his meal out to the veranda. Penny was always there, watching the moonlight, soaking up the stillness. Nothing had changed.

Except everything had.

There was a stillness between them. It was a kind of tension except it wasn't a tension. There was something happening that Matt couldn't figure.

He'd hurt her. He knew he had, he thought, as he sat on the veranda four nights later. He'd seen her face as he'd pulled away that night. She'd practically thrown herself at him. Now she was humiliated and he didn't know what to do about it.

Saying sorry wasn't going to cut it. Saying sorry would simply be saying she'd offered herself to him and he'd refused, but that wasn't how it had been. The tug between them was mutual.

But he'd had no choice. Penny had been honest enough to accept their desire was mutual, but the barriers he'd put up over the years had held. He wasn't going down that path again.

But what path? The path of grief he'd felt when

his mother had left? When the old man who'd befriended him had died?

Or the path of betrayal both his mother and his wife had shown him?

He'd put Penny in the same bracket and she knew it. He'd humiliated her. He'd hurt her. He knew it but he didn't have a clue what to do about it.

And maybe Penny was used to such humiliation because she simply got on with it. She smiled at him, she used the same casual banter, she sat on the veranda now and shared the silence and it was as if nothing had happened.

Except the hurt was still there. How did he know? The sparkle of fun behind her eyes had changed, just a little. She was good at hiding hurt, he thought. If he didn't know her so well…

How did he know her so well? He didn't have a clue. He only knew that he did and he also knew that it had him retreating.

If he went one step further…

He couldn't. The next step would be a crashing down of those boundaries. A shattering of armour.

After all those years, how could he do that?

Penny rose. They'd been sitting on the veranda for only twenty minutes or so and they usually stayed an hour, but tomorrow was the last day of the shear. He had things to do and maybe she did too.

Or maybe this thing between them was too much.

'I'm making bulk choc chip cookies before I go to bed,' she told him. 'The team's heading on to McLarens' tomorrow and they're already whinging about the cooking they'll get there. I thought I'd send them with a goodbye kit.'

'They'll expect you back next year,' Matt told her and she paused and looked down at him in the dim light.

'I'll be well into organizing my catering company by then,' she said thoughtfully. 'But if you pay me enough I'll come.'

'Is that what you plan to do? Set up a catering company?'

'Yes,' she said, almost as if she was speaking to herself. 'I'll make it a success. I know it. Maybe I can find enough competent staff interested in outback experiences to let me offer catering for shearing.'

And he had to ask. 'So will you come, or will it be your competent staff?'

'Who knows?' She said it lightly but he still heard the pain.

'Penny?'

'Mmm?' She leaned down to lift his empty plate from the bench beside him but he reached out and took her wrist before she could lift it.

'Are you staying for the next two weeks?' he asked. 'You haven't said.'

She stilled. She looked down at her wrist.

He released it. No pressure.

What was he thinking, no pressure? There was pressure everywhere.

'Do you still want me to?'

And of course he should say no. He should say the thought had been a dumb one when he'd made the offer. His barricades needed reinforcing.

He'd hurt her and he had no intention of hurting her again. He needed to back off and let her go.

But the night was still and Penny didn't move. His grip on her wrist was light. She could pull away if she wanted.

She didn't.

And all at once he thought: *To hell with barricades. Let's just...see.*

'This thing between us…' he managed and she stayed silent. What happened next was obviously down to him. As it should be.

'Penny, the way I feel…it's been so long. And, to be honest…' He shook his head and finally released her wrist. 'Penny, you've been hurt. You know how it feels. But me?'

And then he stopped. How could he explain? How could he tell anyone the hurt of those long years?

But then he thought this was Penny and he'd hurt her. He couldn't let it stay like this. He needed to let down the barricades a little.

He needed to talk.

'If you don't want to tell me, you don't need to,' she said gently.

She was giving him an out. Her generosity almost took his breath away, and it tore away the last of his reservations.

She sat beside him, as if she understood he needed time. He couldn't look at her. For some reason it seemed impossible to say what had to be said when he was watching her.

But her body was touching his and the warmth of her, her closeness—her trust?—made it imperative to tell her what he'd told nobody. Ever.

And finally he did.

'Penny, my mother was a serial relationship disaster,' he said at last. 'She went from man to man to man. Every time she fell deeply, irrevocably in love, and every single relationship meant our lives were turned upside down. Romance for my mother inevitably ended in chaos and heartbreak. Moving houses, moving schools, debt collectors, sometimes even assault, hospitals, the courts. The best thing Mum ever did for me was run from a calamitous relationship and take the housekeeping job on Sam's farm. That was my salvation. If she hadn't done that, heaven knows where I'd have been. Sam's farm was my first and only taste of stability and I stayed there for ten years. Sam left me the farm and I thought I'd stay there for ever. And then I discovered the bauxite and Darrilyn discovered me.'

'More chaos?' Penny whispered. She was looking out at the moonlight too, giving him space. Giving him silence to work out what he needed to say.

'More chaos,' he said grimly. 'I was naïve, little more than an idiot kid, and I was besotted. I didn't put the discovery of bauxite and the sudden interest of the neighbouring farmer's gorgeous daughter together. I married her and when we found out she was pregnant I was over the moon. But marriage and pregnancy had been her only goals. Legally, they gave her the right to the money she wanted. She headed to the US with a guy who knew her worth and was probably in on her plan from the beginning. So that's it. I see Lily twice a year and it breaks my heart.'

'But now?' She sounded as if she was walking on eggshells. 'You said she might be coming home.'

'Home?' He gave a hollow laugh. 'Does she have such a thing? Her mother's relationships have broken down again and again. Lily's been given the same raw deal as me, but there's nothing I can do about it. Her mother's always refused to let her come to Australia. I leave the farm with the boys twice a year and spend as much time with her as I can, and every time I leave it rips me in two. But even if I moved there Darrilyn wouldn't give me more access. So that's it, Penny. That's where I've been with relationships. Burned. I don't need them.'

'So…' Penny took a deep breath '…Matt, what's that got to do with me?'

'I don't know.' And it was an honest answer. How could he explain what he didn't understand himself? 'Penny, how I feel…'

'Must be like I feel,' she ventured when he couldn't go on. 'Like I've been an idiot and how can I trust myself to try again? Only your ghosts must be harder on you than mine. My parents have their faults but they've given me stability.' Her gaze raked the moonlit landscape. 'You know, this is the most settled place I've ever been in. I'm imagining how you must have felt as a child when you finally made it to Sam's farm. And now. Here's your home and life is good. You wouldn't want to mess with that for anything.'

'You mean I wouldn't want to mess with that for you?'

'I'm not putting words into your mouth,' she said with sudden asperity. She rose, breaking the moment, and a tinge of anger entered her voice. 'I can't help you, Matt. I have my own demons to deal with and, believe me, the fact that I've been monumentally dumb is a huge thing to accept. I don't need a relationship either.' She took a deep breath as if she was having trouble forcing the words out, but finally she managed it.

'But you know what? Regardless of relationships, I'm moving on. Being here has kept my demons at bay, regardless of…of what's happening between us. And I still have the same problem—media interest in my appalling sister and her equally appalling fiancé. I like working here,' she confessed. 'It feels good and I suspect if I made a pile of meals and stocked the freezer, you guys would be grateful.'

'We would.' He definitely would.

'There you go, then. Maybe that's my bottom line. There's cooking to be done and organization in the house. I can put my head down and go for it.'

'I don't want you to work…'

'I'm staying to work, Matt,' she said, still with that trace of astringency. 'Anything else…who knows? As I said, we each have our own demons. But should they affect the next two weeks? Maybe not. So let's make this an employment contract only. Two more weeks of work—at shearers' cook rates.'

'Hey! You're not cooking for a team. Shearers' cook rates?' But he felt himself starting to smile.

She arched her brows and met his gaze head-on. 'I'm filling the freezer and that'll be like cooking for a team. Shearers' cook rates or nothing. That's my offer, Matt Fraser, and it's final. So…do you still want me to stay or do you not?'

She was looking up at him, resolute, courageous, firm.

When he'd first met her he'd thought she was ditzy. She wasn't. She had intelligence to spare.

YOUR PARTICIPATION IS REQUESTED!

Dear Reader,

Since you are a lover of our books – we would like to get to know you!

Inside you will find a short Reader's Survey. Sharing your answers with us will help our editorial staff understand who you are and what activities you enjoy.

To thank you for your participation, we would like to send you 2 books and 2 gifts – **ABSOLUTELY FREE!**

Enjoy your gifts with our appreciation,

Pam Powers

**SEE INSIDE
FOR READER'S
SURVEY**

For Your Reading Pleasure...

We'll send you 2 books and 2 gifts
ABSOLUTELY FREE
just for completing our Reader's Survey!

YOURS FREE!
We'll send you two fabulous surprise gifts absolutely FREE, just for trying our books!

Visit us at:
www.ReaderService.com

YOUR READER'S SURVEY
"THANK YOU" FREE GIFTS INCLUDE:
▶ **2 FREE books**
▶ **2 lovely surprise gifts**

◀ **DETACH AND MAIL CARD TODAY!** ▶

PLEASE FILL IN THE CIRCLES COMPLETELY TO RESPOND

1) What type of fiction books do you enjoy reading? (Check all that apply)
○ Suspense/Thrillers   ○ Action/Adventure   ○ Modern-day Romances
○ Historical Romance   ○ Humor   ○ Paranormal Romance

2) What attracted you most to the last fiction book you purchased on impulse?
○ The Title   ○ The Cover   ○ The Author   ○ The Story

3) What is usually the greatest influencer when you <u>plan</u> to buy a book?
○ Advertising   ○ Referral   ○ Book Review

4) How often do you access the internet?
○ Daily ○ Weekly ○ Monthly ○ Rarely or never

5) How many NEW paperback fiction novels have you purchased in the past 3 months?
○ 0 - 2   ○ 3 - 6   ○ 7 or more

YES! I have completed the Reader's Survey. Please send me the 2 FREE books and 2 FREE gifts (gifts are worth about $10 retail) for which I qualify. I understand that I am under no obligation to purchase any books, as explained on the back of this card.

119/319 HDL GLNV

FIRST NAME	LAST NAME

ADDRESS

APT.#	CITY

STATE/PROV.	ZIP/POSTAL CODE

Offer limited to one per household and not applicable to series that subscriber is currently receiving.
Your Privacy—The Reader Service is committed to protecting your privacy. Our Privacy Policy is available online at www.ReaderService.com or upon request from the Reader Service. We make a portion of our mailing list available to reputable third parties that offer products we believe may interest you. If you prefer that we not exchange your name with third parties, or if you wish to clarify or modify your communication preferences, please visit us at www.ReaderService.com/consumerschoice or write to us at Reader Service Preference Service, P.O. Box 9062, Buffalo, NY 14240-9062. Include your complete name and address.

HR-217-SUR17

© 2016 ENTERPRISES LIMITED
® and ™ are trademarks owned and and used by the trademark owner and/or its licensee. Printed in the U.S.A.

READER SERVICE—Here's how it works:

Accepting your 2 free Harlequin® Romance Larger Print books and 2 free gifts (gifts valued at approximately $10.00) places you under no obligation to buy anything. You may keep the books and gifts and return the shipping statement marked "cancel." If you do not cancel, about a month later we'll send you 4 additional books and bill you just $5.34 each in the U.S. or $5.74 each in Canada. That is a savings of at least 15% off the cover price. It's quite a bargain! Shipping and handling is just 50¢ per book in the U.S. and 75¢ per book in Canada.* You may cancel at any time, but if you choose to continue, every month we'll send you 4 more books, which you may either purchase at the discount price plus shipping and handling or return to us and cancel your subscription. *Terms and prices subject to change without notice. Prices do not include applicable taxes. Sales tax applicable in N.Y. Canadian residents will be charged applicable taxes. Offer not valid in Quebec. Books received may not be as shown. All orders subject to approval. Credit or debit balances in a customer's account(s) may be offset by any other outstanding balance owed by or to the customer. Please allow 4 to 6 weeks for delivery. Offer available while quantities last.

▲ If offer card is missing write to: Reader Service, P.O. Box 1867, Buffalo, NY 14240-1867 or visit www.ReaderService.com ▲

BUSINESS REPLY MAIL
FIRST-CLASS MAIL   PERMIT NO. 717   BUFFALO, NY

POSTAGE WILL BE PAID BY ADDRESSEE

READER SERVICE
PO BOX 1867
BUFFALO NY 14240-9952

NO POSTAGE
NECESSARY
IF MAILED
IN THE
UNITED STATES

She was beautiful.

Suddenly he wondered—was this the courage to try again?

And then there was no choice. The night righted itself. He rose and took her hands.

'Penny, I want you to stay.'

'Really?'

'Really.'

'Then I accept. I'm on a great wage. You have big freezers and I like a challenge. What's not to love?'

What's not to love?

It was all he could do not to kiss her. And then he thought: *Why not?*

So he did and, amazingly, wonderfully, she didn't object. She responded.

But this wasn't the kiss of passion they'd shared on the night of the owls. It was tentative—a question—and when they pulled apart the question was still in their eyes.

'You know, when you're around I have trouble being interested in how empty my freezers are,' he confessed.

'Well, you should be.' She was smiling as she stepped back. She seemed suddenly a woman in charge of her world, ready to move on. 'Because you're paying me heaps.' She tugged her hands back and he let her go. 'For the rest, let's just see. But for now... Matt, I need to go bake some cookies. Freezers, here I come.'

* * *

He headed out to check on the last pens of sheep, the last runs before the end of shearing.

Penny headed for the kitchen.

She'd promised the shearing team takeaway choc chip cookies. Right. She could do that.

Samson snoozed by the fire. The kitchen felt like a refuge.

She mixed her two flours and then stared at the mixture and stared at the flour sacks and wondered—had she just used half self-raising flour, half plain, or had she put in two lots of plain?

Uh oh.

She started again, this time trusting herself so little that she made a list of ingredients that were usually in her head and ticked them as she put them in.

But how could she think of ingredients?

Matt had kissed her. Twice. Matt wanted her to stay.

And she understood him. From that first day when she'd seen him on his gorgeous black horse she'd thought of him as a man in charge of his world, and little had happened to change that. The shearers looked up to him and it wasn't because he owned the place. She'd learned enough of human nature now to know bosses earned respect; they didn't buy it.

So Matt was a man of strength, intelligence and

honour, but she'd just been allowed a glimpse of the building blocks that had made him. It felt like an enormous privilege.

She put both her hands in the bowl and started mixing. The feel of the cookie dough under her hands was a comfort. It was a task she'd loved doing for years.

The family cook had taught her to do this. Her parents hadn't been around much but they'd been in the background.

Who'd baked choc chip cookies for Matt?

No one. She knew it as surely as she knew what he'd told her was scarcely the tip of the iceberg that was the nightmare of his childhood.

'Bless you, Sam,' she told the old farmer who'd finally taken the young Matt under his wing. 'I wish I could make you choc chip cookies.'

And suddenly her eyes filled with tears. Why? It hardly made sense. She sniffed and told herself she was a dope but the tears kept coming.

'So we're adding a little salty water into the mix,' she said out loud. 'My secret ingredient.'

Two weeks to cure a lifetime of hurt?

That wasn't the way it worked. Matt didn't see himself as someone who needed curing, and she was hardly qualified to help.

'But he might kiss me again...'

The tears disappeared. Hope was suddenly all around her, a bright, perky little voice that bounced with delight. Enough with the past. She had freezers to fill.

And demons to scatter?

'I hope he likes choc chip cookies,' she told the sleeping Samson. 'Because I'm about to fill his freezers with a ton.'

He'd hired her for two more weeks. He'd told her his past.

Was he nuts?

He checked the pens and then walked down the paddocks to check the newly shorn sheep. The weather was brilliant, as it had been for the whole shear. The starkly white sheep didn't even appear to notice that they'd lost their coats. They were relaxed, hardly edging away as he walked the boundaries of the holding paddocks. There were no problems with the flock that he could see. No problems on the horizon either.

He opened the gates of the house paddocks to the pastures beyond. To all intents and purposes, the sheep were free.

Like he intended to be.

Freedom. That was what he'd craved when he'd somehow hauled himself together after Darrilyn walked out. His mother had moved from one hysterical mess to another. He'd spent his childhood dealing with her tears, her drama, her hopelessness, and his one foray into marriage had been more of the same.

Freedom had looked good. This place was his solace, his refuge, his love.

But now? Not only had he just opened himself up to Penny, exposing pain he'd never thought he'd reveal, but he'd pushed her to stay for two weeks.

And a question was starting to niggle.

Did he have the courage to try again? With a pink princess with a past almost as troubled as his?

He walked on. In the distance he could still see the house. The lights were on at the south end, which meant the kitchen was still in use. Penny would be cooking.

He could go and join her. He could sit at the kitchen table and watch her hands create food to die for. He could watch the flour accumulate on her nose—she always seemed to have flour on her nose.

Maybe he could offer to help—he could wash while she wiped.

There was a romantic thought.

He stopped and closed his eyes. The silence was almost absolute. Even the owls were silent and he thought suddenly: *It's as if something momentous is about to happen.*

Momentous? Like Matt Fraser breaks his own rule and lets his guard down with a woman?

How insulting was that? he thought, and swore

silently to himself. What was he expecting, that Penny jump him? That he'd have to fight her off?

It was a dumb thought, but it had its merits. He found himself smiling as he walked on. He wouldn't mind.

He wouldn't fight her off.

'I won't hurt her.' There was another thought, almost a vow.

How serious was he getting, and how fast?

'Not serious at all,' he told himself as he finally turned for home. Surely she'd finished cooking by now? The house would be in darkness and he could slip in without seeing her.

Was that what he wanted? To avoid her for two weeks?

'You know it's not or you wouldn't have invited her,' he told himself and he found himself wishing his dogs were with him. His own company wasn't cutting it. But the dogs were exhausted after a full day in the yards.

So was he. He needed to go to sleep and stop worrying about what lay ahead.

And stop fancying what else might happen.

'When are you coming home?'

Penny's mother hadn't phoned her for two weeks. When she didn't phone, Penny knew she was in trouble. Depression dogged her mother, and silence was a symptom. But Louise's silence while Brett and Felicity outlined their marriage plans had made Penny decide enough was enough.

Penny's father was a bully and her half-sister was a self-serving shrew, but Louise didn't have the courage to stand up to either of them.

Tonight her mother's voice sounded thick with tears. Penny was willing herself not to care.

It didn't work. How could she stop caring?

'I told you, Mum, I'm working out here. It doesn't matter when I get home.'

'Where exactly are you working?'

'South Australia. Murray River country. I'm working as a cook, Mum. I'm safe, I'm doing a good job and I'm keeping...' She paused, but why not say it like it was? 'I'm keeping myself occupied so I don't need to think about Felicity and Brett.'

'They're both unhappy about hurting you.'

'You know, I'm very sure they're not.'

'No, they are.' And here she went again, Penny thought. Her mother spent her life pretending they were happy families. 'I'm sure Felicity would like you to be her bridesmaid.'

'I'm sure she'd hate it.'

'Well, she *should* have you.' The tears were un-mistakable now. 'I don't like you unhappy. I want you to be her bridesmaid and I told her that.'

'It's not going to happen,' Penny said gently. 'I wish Felicity all the best but I'm not coming home for the wedding.'

'Not even coming?' Her mother sounded appalled.

'Mum, how can I?'

'Sweetheart, you must.' Her mother hiccupped on a sob. 'It's in three weeks. St Barnabas Chapel followed by a grand reception on the Harbour. For you not to be there…' Another sob. 'Felicity's mother will lord it over me. Your father won't care. Penny, I can't do it without you.'

How impossible was it to harden your heart? She tried. 'Mum, I'm happy here.'

There was a moment's pause. Maybe something in Penny's voice had got through. 'Really?'

'I am,' she told her. 'And Samson's turning into a sheepdog. You should see him.'

'I thought you were working at a hotel.'

'This is sheep country.'

'So you're meeting the locals?'

'I…some of them. But Mum, I can't come to the wedding. I'm so busy I'm even starting to forget what Felicity and Brett did to me.' She took a deep breath and decided to say it like it was. 'To be honest, I'm even starting to feel sorry for Felicity. And worried. You should tell Felicity there are a lot nicer men than Brett.'

'You wanted to marry him.'

'That was before I knew what a toerag he was. There are still some honourable men in the world.'

She shouldn't have said it. If there was one thing

Louise was good at, it was sussing out gossip and, despite her distress, she could almost feel her mother's antennae quiver. "'Honourable men",' she said slowly. There was a loaded pause and then, 'Penny, have you met one?'

Shut up, Penny, she told herself. Get off the phone fast.

But she wouldn't lie. Had she met an honourable man? Yes, she had, and the thought was a good one.

'That's for me to know and you to guess,' she told her mother, forcing herself to sound breezy. 'Goodnight, Mum.'

'Penny, please come.'

'I can't.'

But she lay in bed that night and thought of her mother's tears. She thought of her mother, isolated at the wedding by her appalling husband and her even more appalling stepdaughter.

How did you rid yourself of the ties of loving?

She should ask Matt.

CHAPTER EIGHT

IN THE NEXT few days, while Matt coped with the tasks that had to be done before the wool was sent for sale, Penny attacked the house.

If anyone had ever told her she'd find joy in a mop and bucket, she'd have told them they were crazy. But cleaning took her mind off her mother's increasingly distressed phone calls, and this was a challenge worth tackling.

Ever since she'd walked into the house she'd thought of it as something out of a Charles Dickens novel. 'I feel like I might find Miss Havisham under one of these dust sheets,' she told Matt as they sat on the veranda that night. 'How long have they been here?'

'Donald's mother was a socialite,' Matt told her. 'She ran away when Donald was seven and his dad pretty much closed the house. When Donald sold me the house and contents I left it as it was. I use my bedroom, the den and the kitchen. I've no need for anything else.'

'You're two male versions of Miss Havisham,' she told him. 'Not that I mind. You can gloat over your wool clip while I clean. I'll even enjoy it.'

'I would be grateful,' Matt admitted. 'If Lily comes...'

'Is that likely to happen?'

'Maybe,' he said slowly. 'She's not getting on with Darrilyn's new partner. Darrilyn's talking about sending her to school in Australia so it's not impossible.' But he sounded like a man who was scarcely allowing himself to hope.

'Does she know anyone in Australia?'

'No, and that's why I'm telling Darrilyn she'd need to come here first. So she knows some sort of base.'

'Poor kid,' Penny said, and meant it. She knew all about being a teenage thorn in her socialite parents' lives and the thought of the unknown Lily was part of her driving force.

'The sofa in the main sitting room's so hard it feels like sitting on bricks,' she told him. 'Why not replace it with something squishy? Now the flood's receded you can get it delivered and, with the fire lit, that room would be lovely. It needs a big telly, though, and all the things that go with it. If Lily comes she won't feel welcome if she has to sit on a horsehair brick. And her bedroom...I'd suggest buying a four-poster bed. Not pink, unless you see her as a pink girl.'

'I don't,' he said faintly. 'Penny, she probably won't come.'

'You know,' she said diffidently, 'if I was thirteen and there was conflict at home, my dad sending pictures of the bedroom he'd prepared for me might well make me feel a whole lot better about myself, whether I was allowed to come or not.'

'Even if they're never used?'

'You can afford it,' she told him bluntly. 'And Lily sounds like she needs it.'

'How do you know?'

'I don't. I'm guessing. You want to go with my guess or with yours?'

He looked at her for a long moment and then raked his hair. 'You probably do know more about thirteen-year-old girls than I do.'

'Hey, I was one once,' she said cheerfully. 'If you agree, I'd suggest we go with a theme of antique white. The rooms are so old-fashioned, why don't we...'

'We?'

'Me then,' she said and grinned. 'Why don't I go for white on white? Broderie anglaise, heritage quilting, a deep rug on the floor, some old-fashioned sampler type pictures on the wall...'

'How do you know what she'd like?'

'I know what I'd like,' she told him. 'If my parents had done something like this for me...'

And then her voice cracked. She heard it but there wasn't a thing she could do about it.

'Still hurting, huh?' Matt said. They were sitting on the edge of the veranda and he reached out and touched her face. It was a fleeting gesture, but it said, in some deep way, that he understood the distress she still felt whenever she thought of her mother's pleas. The knowledge was enough to make her toes curl.

She concentrated fiercely on getting them uncurled.

'I can forget about it here,' she managed.

'But you can't stay here for ever?'

'No. And Malley's isn't an option any more. But neither is staying away, I guess. My sister's getting married on the seventeenth and Mum's organising a family dinner on the twelfth. On Dad's orders. To heal differences, he says, and he expects me to be there. He'll blame Mum if I'm not.'

'Surely you won't go?' He sounded appalled. That was how she felt but what choice did she have?

'You see, I love Mum,' she said simply.

She loved, therefore she did what was expected.

Matt was silent for a while. The night was closing in on them and somehow it felt…almost threatening? Why did this man make her feel so exposed?

'I guess that's why I don't love,' Matt said at last. 'I won't let myself need people and I won't be needed.'

'No?' She gave a hollow laugh. 'What about Lily?'

'Lily's different. She's my kid.'

'And this is my mum.'

'And your mum should be protecting you, as I'd protect Lily. Penny, your mum's an adult. She's had a lifetime to form her own armour and maybe that's what you need to do.'

'That's cruel.'

'It is,' he said gently. 'But your mother's made her own choices and maybe it's time for you to do the same. You only have one life. Will you spend it trying to please your family? Being a doormat?'

'What's the alternative? Carrying a bucketload of guilt for the rest of my life?' She tried to say it lightly but failed.

'So you'll go back to your mum.'

'I might.' But she knew she would.

'Maybe your mum could come to you?'

'What, here?'

'Maybe not. It'd be a bit of a culture shock— from Sydney to Jindalee.' She heard Matt's smile rather than saw it. They hadn't turned on the veranda lights and the darkness had crept up on their silence. 'But Penny, if you make yourself a life, set up your catering company, do what you want to do… If your mum wants, then maybe she could choose to help you? Maybe she could live near you, on her own rather than in an unhappy marriage? You could help her on your terms rather than hers.'

'She'll never leave.'

'Then that's her choice,' he said gently. 'But it doesn't have to be your choice. Attending the wedding should be your line in the sand. Maybe you should do something for yourself instead. Have a weekend in a fabulous resort. I'll arrange it for you if you like, as a thank you for getting me out of such trouble at shearing. But, no matter what, just say no.'

'Oh, Matt…'

'You can do it,' he growled and he rose and leant down and ran a finger lightly through her curls. The touch made her shiver. 'If you can keep a mob of shearers happy, you can do anything. I believe in you, Penny Hindmarsh-Firth, so maybe it's time for you to believe in yourself.'

And then there was another of those silences which fell between them so often. Mostly they felt natural. Mostly they felt good. But this one…

This one seemed loaded.

You can do it. That was what Matt had said.

Do what? What she really wanted?

If she really believed in herself, Penny thought, she'd get up from where she was sitting and she'd kiss this guy senseless. She might even demand he let go of his own ghosts and come to this luxury resort with her.

But she was Penny. Asking for love? She never had. She'd loved and loved and where had that got her?

You can do it.

Yeah, right. Not in a million years.

'Goodnight, Penny,' Matt said heavily then, as

if he too acknowledged the impossibility of moving on.

'Goodnight,' she whispered.

She felt sad. No, she felt desolate, but still she went inside and rang her mother. She said no and she meant it—and, despite the weird feeling of desolation, it felt like a beginning.

Two days later, the year's wool clip was finally loaded for market. She saw the slump of Matt's shoulders as he watched the line of trucks roll off the property. She thought of the work he'd put in, the late nights he'd pulled, the light on in his study until almost dawn.

And suddenly she thought…picnic?

She walked out to meet him in the driveway.

'Well done,' she told him.

'The fleece is great. It feels a whole lot better than taking money from a bauxite mine.'

'I'll bet it does,' she said and then added diffidently, 'Want to come on a picnic?'

'What?' It was as if he hadn't heard the word before.

'You haven't stopped for weeks,' she told him. 'Ron and Harv are rested. They can take over anything that needs to be done. Is there anywhere we can go? Somewhere you can't see a single sheep? Honest, Matt, you must be seeing them in your sleep.'

'If I fell asleep every time I counted them I'd be in trouble,' he agreed, smiling faintly. 'But now I need to get onto drenching.'

'Matt. One day. Holiday. Picnic.'

And he turned and looked at her. 'You must be exhausted too.'

'If it'll make you agree to a picnic, yes, I am.'

She met his gaze, tilted her chin, almost daring him to refuse.

Finally he seemed to relent. 'There is somewhere...' he said doubtfully. 'But we'd have to take horses. The ground's undermined by rabbit warrens and the four-wheel drive won't get in there without damaging the ferns.'

'And we don't want that,' she said, not having a clue what he was talking about but prepared to encourage him. And then she thought about it a bit more and said, less enthusiastically, 'Horses?'

'Do you ride?'

'My mother bought me a pony when I was seven,' she said, feeling more and more dubious. 'It was fat and it didn't go any more than a dozen steps before it needed a nap. So I know which side to get on and I'm not too bad at sitting. Anything else is beyond me. Is there anywhere else we can go?'

'I have a horse who'll fit the bill,' he said cheerfully and her heart sank.

'Really?'

'Maisie's thirty. Sam bought her for me when I was twelve, and I loved her. She and I ruled the land but she has become rather fat. And lazy. But she'll follow Nugget to the ends of the earth. It'll be like sitting on a rocking chair.'

But she'd been distracted from the horse.

'Why do I keep loving your Sam more and more?' she whispered. 'He bought the son of his housekeeper a horse?'

'Yeah, he did,' Matt told her and his voice softened too. 'He changed my life.'

'Would he tell you to go on a picnic?'

'I guess…maybe.'

'Then let's do it,' she told him. 'As long as I can borrow one of the living room cushions. How far is it?'

'It'll take about an hour.'

'Two hours there and back?' She took a deep breath and then looked up at Matt and thought…

'I'll take two cushions,' she told him. 'Let's do it.'

Maisie was a fat old mare, used to spending her days snoozing in the sun and her nights nestled on the straw in Matt's impressive stables. But she perked right up when Matt put the saddle on her, and when Penny tentatively—very tentatively—clambered aboard, she trotted out into the sunshine and sniffed the wind as if she was looking forward to the day as much as Penny.

Matt's two dogs raced furiously ahead, wild with excitement, as if they knew the day would be special. Samson, however, had been racing with them since dawn. He was one tired poodle and he now sat in front of Matt, like the figurehead on the bow of an ancient warship. He looked supremely content and, fifteen minutes into the ride, Penny decided she was too.

The old horse was steady and placid. The day was perfect. Matt rode ahead, looking splendid on his beautiful Nugget. There was little for Penny to think about, or do, for Maisie seemed totally content to follow Nugget. And Matt.

As was Penny. 'I'm with you,' she muttered to Maisie. 'Talk about eye candy. Wow...'

'Sorry?' Matt turned and waited for her to catch up. 'I didn't hear that.'

'You weren't meant to. Maisie and I were communing. I think we're twin souls.'

'I can see that,' he said and grinned and the eye candy meter zipped up into the stratosphere. Matt was wearing jeans and riding boots, and an ancient khaki shirt, open at the throat, sleeves rolled above the elbows. He'd raked his hair too often during shearing and the lanolin from the fleeces had made it look more controlled, coarser. Now, though, the last of the lanolin had been washed away. His hair was ruffled in the warm wind. His face looked relaxed. His deep-set eyes were permanently creased against the sun, but they were smiling. He looked a man at ease.

His horse was magnificent. He looked magnificent.

If I were a Regency heroine I'd be reaching for my smelling salts right now, she thought, and she wanted to tell Maisie because Maisie was watching Nugget with exactly the same look of adoration.

Wait, was she looking at Matt with adoration? She pulled herself up with a jolt.

'You be careful of those saddlebags,' she said, fighting for something prosaic to say. 'I don't want squashed cream puffs.'

'You packed cream puffs?' He'd loaded the cartons of food into his saddlebags without question.

'Why wouldn't I?' she asked with insouciance.

'Why indeed? I thought picnics were sandwiches and apples.'

'Not in my world. Where are we going?'

'We're heading for the hills,' he told her. 'After this rain I'm betting the place we're going will be amazing. I hope I'm right.'

This was his favourite place on the entire property. He'd seen it first the day he'd come to inspect the land. Donald had driven him over the paddocks, shown him the house, the shearing sheds, the outbuildings. He'd shown him the sheep and then he'd driven him here. Donald couldn't make it down the last steep climb. He'd driven him to the top and said, 'There's something down there that's worth a look, boy, if you have the energy to walk down.'

When he did, he'd known that not only would he buy Jindalee, but Jindalee would be his home.

This was his refuge. His quiet place. His place for just…being. Over the years, he and Nugget had forged a track through the undergrowth that was secure enough to get right down to the bottom. He led the way now, slowly and surely, with Maisie plodding behind. He glanced back to tell Penny to hold on tight but he didn't need to. Penny's knees were tight to the saddle. Her hands gripped the kneepads even though her fingers were still light on the reins. She wouldn't take her fear out on Maisie. And now…fear or not, her face reflected pure awe.

The country on this section of the river was so rough, so undermined by underground waterways that no farmer had ever tried to clear it. Now the massive gum trees towered over their heads. The vast, shading canopy meant the understory was an undulating carpet of ferns, a wondrous mat of green that flowed down to the water.

They weren't going all the way to the river. The Murray here was wide and wild, a vast expanse of water where the banks would still be covered with debris from the recent floods. This place was better.

He remembered Donald describing it to him all those years ago.

'There's a place, boy, where one of the creeks flowing underground sneaks up and burbles up over the rocks,' Donald had told him. 'Then it falls and forms a pool bigger'n most swimming pools. You can swim there if you can cope with a bit of cold. It's the cleanest water on God's earth, I swear. And then it slithers through a bed of tumbled rocks and disappears back underground. The ground around is covered with moss. A man can lie on that moss and look up through the gums and see the sky. It's like a slice of heaven.'

Matt had come and seen and fallen in love, and now, as their horses turned into the final clearing, he saw Penny's face and knew she saw it exactly the same way.

'Oh,' she breathed and then fell silent. Awed.

'Not bad, huh?' he said, trying to bite back pride and then he thought: *Why not say it like it is?* 'Best place in the world.'

'Oh, Matt.' She slipped off Maisie and the horse turned to nibble her ear. Her hand automatically went to scratch Maisie's nose. She was a natural horsewoman, Matt thought. He could buy another horse and...

What was he thinking?

The dogs were heading into the ferns, wild with excitement at the smell of rabbits, of something other than sheep, maybe simply at the day itself.

Matt pretty much felt the same—although he surely wasn't thinking of rabbits.

'Can we swim?' she breathed.

'It's icy.'

'But there aren't any…I don't know…crocodiles?'

He grinned. 'No crocodiles.'

'Then I'm in.'

'Did you bring your swimmers?'

'No,' she said and suddenly she was glaring. 'I did not because no one told me that swimming was an option.' She looked again at the waterhole and he saw the moment she made a decision. 'Well,' she said, 'you didn't tell me so you need to face the consequences. My knickers and bra are respectable. You're sure there isn't a posse of photographers behind these trees?'

What sort of world did she live in? 'I'm sure.'

'Don't sound so cocky. They'd be onto you if you didn't have such an ordinary name. You must have kept deliberately under the radar. Matt Fraser? No headlines and I bet you've fought hard to keep it that way. As squillionaire owner of Harriday Holdings, you'd be every women's magazine's Bachelor of the Year, no sweat.'

'So you didn't fight?' he said curiously. 'To keep under the radar?'

'With my father? I was in front of a camera practically before they cut the cord. And with a name like Hindmarsh-Firth it's impossible to duck.'

'So change it.'

'Right,' she said grimly. 'By deed poll? I don't think so. I'd be splashed all over the dailies with *Family Feud* as the headline.' She shrugged. 'No matter. It's all a long way from here and this place is magic. Can I swim?'

'The water's coming straight up from underground. Cold doesn't begin to describe it.'

'You swim here?'

'Yes.'

'But you never bother to pack your bathers when you come here?' Her smile returned. 'I get it. Every respectable squillionaire has his own private swimming pool and this is yours. Can I share?'

'If you dare.'

And she chuckled and tugged her T-shirt off, revealing a sliver of a pink lace bra. 'Of course I dare,' she told him. 'But I'm not doing your naked thing. I happen to be wearing matching knickers and panties—isn't that lucky? Will you join me?'

'I...yes.'

'Then are your boxers respectable, because we Hindmarsh-Firths have our standards?'

He grinned. 'I believe they are—although they're not pink and they're not lace.'

'I don't know what squillionaires are coming to,'

she said, mock serious. 'But I can slum it. Swimming with a guy in cotton boxers? If I must.'

And she turned her back on him, kicked off her shoes, tugged off her jeans—to reveal a pair of knickers that were just as scanty as her bra—and dived straight in.

He'd said it was cold, but this wasn't just cold. This was half a degree above ice. She reached for the rock ledge and gasped and gasped.

And Matt was beside her.

He must have dived in almost as soon as she had. She hadn't noticed him shedding his clothes. She'd been more than a bit embarrassed about the panty-bra thing and had turned her back but now he was beside her.

His arm came out to support her. Maybe he thought her heart might stop.

It felt as if it might stop.

'I told you it was cold,' he said, a trifle smugly, and the iciness of the water and the sudden sensation of his arm around the bare skin of her waist and the smugness in his tone made her want to retort—but how could a girl retort when she was gasping like a fish out of water?

'Oh… Oh…'

'You get used to it if you swim,' he told her. Dammit, his voice wasn't even quavering. Was the man immune?

'This is like those winter plunge ceremonies in the Antarctic,' she stammered and tried to tug herself up to the ledge.

'Penny?'

'Mmm?' She couldn't get a handhold.

'There's a ledge over there that makes it easy to get out, but if you can bear it then try swimming. The cold eases and there's something I want to show you.'

Every nerve ending in her body was screaming for her to get out. But something else was cutting in, overriding the cold of the water.

Matt's arm was around her waist. He'd stripped to his boxers. His body was big and tanned and strong and he was holding her against him.

Was it her imagination or was she warm where she was touching him?

The initial shock was wearing off now—a little. She could breathe again, enough to take in her surroundings.

The pool was magnificent. At one end was a waterfall, not high, maybe head height, but enough to send white water tumbling down over rocks to the pool below. The pool itself was clear and deep, but not so deep that she couldn't see the sandy bottom. Now that she had her breath back she could see tiny slivers of darting fish.

The canopy of trees had parted a little over the pool, so dappled sunlight was playing on the water.

Moss covered the surrounding rocks, and beyond the moss the horses had started grazing. They were obviously appreciating the lush grass in the slice of land where the moss ended and the ferns began.

The scene was idyllic. Enough to make her forget the ice?

Or maybe that was because Matt was beside her. Holding her.

What was a little ice compared to Matt?

'Sh…show me,' she managed through chattering teeth and he grinned.

'Swim first,' he told her. 'Half a dozen fast laps to warm up. Can you do that?'

'Of course. Bossy.'

'I'm not bossy, I'm wise,' he told her. 'Swim or you'll have to get out. Believe me.'

So she swam. The pool was the length of the pool her parents had in their current mansion. She'd spent a lot of time in that pool since the night Brett and Felicity had made their announcement. Swimming was a way she could block out the world.

But she had no intention of blocking the world now, for Matt swam beside her, matching her stroke for stroke. Maybe he wasn't too sure of her ability, she thought. Maybe he thought she might drown if he didn't stick close enough to save her.

Saved by Matt… It was a silly thought but it did something to her insides. The water was still icy but she was warming up, and half of that warming process was Matt. Matt's body inches from hers. Matt's presence. Matt…

They turned in unison and then turned again. Four lengths, five…and then six. She reached the end and grasped the ledge. Matt's arm came around her and held again.

He couldn't think she was drowning now. He was holding her because…?

'Game for the next bit?' he asked and she thought: *With your arm around me I'm game for anything.*

'I…yes.' Her teeth weren't chattering any more. She couldn't say she was warm but the iciness had dropped a notch. The water felt amazing. You could drink this water, she thought, and took a tentative mouthful and it tasted wonderful.

'If the bauxite mine ever fails I can put a bottling factory here and make a mint,' Matt said smugly.

'Don't you dare.'

'Don't worry, I won't,' he told her and he smiled at her again. That smile… It was a caress all by itself.

But he was a man on a mission. He had something to show her.

'The waterfall,' he told her. 'We're going behind it.'

'We are?'

'You can't see anything from out here,' he told her. 'But if you aim to the left of centre, put your head down, hold your breath for thirty seconds and swim right through, you'll find there's a cave.'

'Really?' She stared at the innocent-looking waterfall. 'There's no way I can be trapped?'

He grinned at her note of suspicion. 'You guessed it. You'll find forty-seven skeletons in there, the remains of every single maiden I've ever enticed into my secret lair.'

And she thought suddenly: *How do I know he's not telling the truth?* She'd known him for less than three weeks.

She'd been a fool for Brett. How could she trust her judgement now?

Except this was Matt. And Matt was smiling just a little, teasing.

'I know you're lying,' she told him and he raised a quizzical brow.

'How?'

'Because you couldn't possibly have persuaded forty-seven maidens to jump into this ice.' And she turned towards the waterfall and swam.

It was a weird feeling, to think of swimming through the wall. Instinct told her to reach the tumbling water and stop. She did for a moment, pausing to tread water, feeling the spray of the falls splash on her face.

But Matt was beside her. She could scarcely see him through the mist but he touched her shoulder. 'Here,' he said. 'Straight ahead. Put your head down and swim. It's narrow—you'll feel rocks on either side—but you'll be through in seconds.'

'I…is it dark in there?'

'I promise it's not,' he told her. 'It's safe as houses.'

'Really?'

'Well, not a centrally heated house,' he admitted. 'But it's worth it. Penny, trust me?'

Did she trust him? She stared at him for a long moment. His face was blurred behind the mist of the waterfall but she could still see him. He'd ceased smiling. He was waiting for her to come to a decision—and suddenly it was about more than the trust required to swim through a waterfall.

It was about total trust.

It was about taking a step that felt momentous.

He put out a hand and touched her face, making the rivulets of water stream across his hand rather than across her eyes. Her vision cleared and she saw him as he was.

A loner. A man of strength and courage. Matt.

And something shifted inside her. Something she couldn't name. Something that had never been touched before.

She put out her hand and touched his face back.

'I trust you,' she whispered and he smiled but it was a different kind of smile. It was a smile that said he was in the same unchartered territory as she was.

'Then let's go,' he told her. 'Come on, Penelope Hindmarsh-Firth. Let's do it.'

And he put his hands on her shoulders and twisted her around so she was facing the waterfall and gave her a slight push forward.

'Through you go,' he told her. 'And know that I'm with you all the way.'

Okay, it was scary. The first bit did involve trust. The wash of tumbling water as she swam through was almost enough to push her under, and then she felt the rocks on either side.

Matt had said to swim through. Just keep on going.

She wasn't completely enclosed. She could still surface and breathe if she needed to, though the mist from the falls made that hard. It was a narrow channel through the rocks, and it was getting narrower.

But Matt was behind her. She held her breath and dived like a porpoise.

The rocks on both sides touched her shoulders. She used them to pull herself the last little way.

And emerged...to magic.

It was an underground pool that must feed out somehow into the pool they'd just been in, but at the same level. She could hear the rush of water over her head. The creek must branch, above and below. This pool was roofed, and yet not. There were fissures where the sunlight glimmered through, shafts of golden light making the surface of the underground water glimmer in light and shade.

She could see the canopy of the trees through the fissures, but only glimpses. In a couple of places the water course above was overflowing and spilling down, so rivulets of water splashed the surface of the water in the cavern. Some sort of tiny, pale green creeper was trailing downward, tendril after tendril of soft, lush vine.

And at the edges were flat rock ledges. It was, as Matt had said, totally safe.

It took her breath away.

She trod water and turned and Matt was right behind her. Watching her. And the expression on his face... He loved this place, she thought.

'Oh, Matt, it's beautiful,' she breathed, and he smiled, an odd little smile she'd never seen before.

'Beautiful,' he agreed, and the way he said it... It took her breath away all over again.

'I...do you come here often?' She sounded nervous, she thought, and maybe she was, but in a weird way. It was as if the world was holding its breath. Something seemed about to happen and she wasn't sure what.

'Just when I need to,' he told her. 'Even Donald doesn't know about this secret place. Isn't it great?'

'It is,' she breathed. 'So...your forty-seven maidens?'

'Okay, I made 'em up.' They were treading water. If they swam a couple of yards further on they could stand, but for some reason that seemed dangerous. 'The water above doesn't run except in times of flooding, so the waterfall's a rare thing. But this underground cavern's always here. You're the first person I've ever brought here.'

'That sounds…momentous.'

'I think it is,' he said seriously. 'Penny?'

'Mmm?' What else was a woman to say?

'I'd like to kiss you.'

And suddenly she wasn't cold at all. She was exceedingly warm.

Apart from her body.

'I'm all for it,' she told him. 'Except that I can't feel my toes and if I kiss you I might forget about them and I'll get frostbite from the toes up.'

'Ever the practical…'

'Someone has to be,' she told him and only she knew what a struggle it was to say it. 'But I have a suggestion.'

'Which is?'

'That we swim back through that waterfall, we get ourselves dry and then we think about kissing.'

There was a moment's pause. 'You mean we have an agenda?'

'I think it's more than an agenda,' she told him, and smiled and smiled. 'Agendas can be changed.

The time for agendas is past. Consider the kiss a promise.'

'Then one for the road,' he told her and he tugged her forward and kissed her, as long and as deeply as two people treading ice-cold water could manage.

And then they turned to the sheen of white water that marked the entrance to their tiny piece of paradise and swam right through.

Back to where the horses were waiting. Back to where their picnic was waiting.

Back to the promise of a kiss and so much more.

Matt produced a towel and insisted on drying her. He rubbed her body until she could feel her toes again, until her body was glowing pink, until the feel of his hands rubbing her dry started sending messages to her brain she had no hope of fighting.

Who'd want to fight?

Then he gathered her to him and he kissed her as she'd never been kissed before.

His skin was still damp, but out of the water the sun did the drying for him. And who was worried about a little damp? He felt almost naked and her tiny wisps of lace hardly seemed to exist.

She melted into him. His mouth claimed hers, her body moulded to his and the kiss lasted an eternity.

But of course it couldn't.

'Dammit, I should have...' he said at last, putting her away from him with what seemed an al-most superhuman effort.

'So should I,' she told him, knowing exactly what he was talking about. 'I packed sandwiches, cream puffs, wine, chocolate. I can't believe I for-got the After-Picnic essentials.'

'It wouldn't have been After-Picnic,' he told her and tugged her forward again. This kiss was even better. Longer. Deeper.

This was a kiss that had a language all its own. It was a kiss that promised a future.

It was a kiss that sent her senses into some sort of orbit.

But finally sense prevailed—as did hunger. They attacked the picnic basket as if there was no tomor-row—indeed, for now it seemed as if tomorrow wasn't on the horizon. And then they lay back on the moss and gazed up through the canopy at the sky above.

We might just as well have made love, Penny thought dreamily. She was held close in the crook of Matt's arm. They hadn't bothered dressing—with the warmth of the sun there was no need, and to put any barrier at all between them seemed wrong. She was warm, she was sated, the ride and the swim had made her sleepy…

'Penny?'

'Mmm?' It was hard to get her voice to work.

'How heartbroken are you about Brett?'

Brett. He seemed a million miles away. Part of another life.

If it hadn't been for Felicity, she'd be married by now, she thought, and it was enough to wake her up completely. She shuddered.

Matt tugged her tighter. The warmth of him was insulation against pain, but then she thought: *There's no pain.*

Humiliation, though, that was a different matter.

'There's no need to be jealous,' she told him.

'Hey, I'm not jealous.' She could hear the smile in his voice. 'I've got the girl. Whoever Brett's holding now, he's welcome. No one can match the woman I have in my arms.'

It took her breath away, even more than the icy water had. The statement was so immense…

And it was the truth. She heard it in his voice and part of her wanted to weep. Or sing. Or both.

Instead, she twisted herself up so she could kiss him again. He kissed her back but then tugged her close, held her tight and said again, 'Talk about Brett.'

'Why do you want to know?'

'Because he's important,' he told her. 'Because he made you run. Because your family's important to you and I figure if they're important to you then maybe I need to know about them. So Brett seems a way in.'

And there was a statement to take her breath

away all over again. He wanted… No, he hadn't said wanted… He needed to know about them.

He was talking of the future?

So tell him.

'It was dumb,' she told him. 'I was dumb. I'm a people pleaser. My family's nothing if not volatile and my father's a bully. My half-sister's an airhead but she also has a temper. My mum…' She hesitated. 'She might seem like an airhead too, but she's not. Maybe underneath she's like me. She tries to keep us all happy. But she won't stand up to Dad. She never has. She just tries to smooth things over, to present the perfect appearance to the outside world. And somewhere along the line I learned to go along with her. Keep the peace. Make them happy.'

'So… Brett?'

'I was cooking in London,' she told him. 'I seldom went home—to be honest, as little as possible because Dad hates what I do and he gives me a hard time. But Mum rang me every night. Things seemed okay. But then Grandma died—Mum's mother—and I hadn't realized how much Mum needed her. Like she needs me. It's weird but being needed seems to be hardwired into us. Grandma supported Mum any way she could, which gave Mum the strength to stay in an awful marriage. When Grandma died she fell apart.' Penny sighed. 'Anyway, I came home and Dad pushed and

pushed me into the PR job and I was so scared
for Mum that finally I said yes. And what a disaster. I must have been depressed too, or at least my
radar for slimeballs was depressed because Brett
found me easy pickings. I was the daughter of the
man he wanted to schmooze. Only, of course, he
misjudged. He hadn't figured the family dynamics
until it was too late—that Felicity is Dad's favourite. But then Felicity came home and he figured
it out and the rest is history.'

'He's an idiot.'

She thought about that for a while. It was odd,
but lying here on the moss, held hard against such
a man as Matt...her perspective changed. Somehow the fog of humiliation that had been with her
since that appalling dinner suddenly cleared, va-
porising into the filtered sunlight and the shadows
of the gums above her head.

'He's not an idiot,' she said softly. 'He's a lying,
scheming toad who thinks he can get near Dad's
fortune by marrying into the family. And maybe
he can, and yes, he now has the beautiful daughter,
but what he hasn't reckoned on is Felicity's temper.
Felicity's hysterics. He doesn't know what it's like
to live with Felicity. I wish him joy.'

'Punishment enough?'

'You said it,' she said softly. 'And now...I'm here
with you. I still worry about Mum but, as you said,
there's no way I can fix her problems for her.'

'Not when there're cream puffs and waterholes and sheep…'

And there it was again. That suggestion of a future.

'No indeed,' she said and smiled, because how could she not? She kissed him again because there was no choice in that either. 'Brett and Felicity are no longer in my world. I think, right now, I could even face their wedding. But you're right, I won't.'

And then Samson, who'd been sleeping on the edge of the clearing in between Matt's two dogs, suddenly decided he needed a little of his mistress's attention. He edged forward to wiggle between them, and suddenly they were both laughing.

'Right now my world seems to smell of sheep,' she said happily, even joyfully. 'And eau de rabbit burrow and damp dog. And is there horse dung in the mixture as well? And you know what? I love it. Just for now, Matt Fraser, I am a very happy woman. Brett and Felicity can have my old world. For now I'm happy in this one.'

CHAPTER NINE

THE NEXT WEEK passed in a blur of hard work and happiness. Matt was pressuring her to slow down, to give herself a break after the exertion of shearing, but why would she?

She made the house pristine. The orders for the new furniture were coming in, to be admired, placed, enjoyed. She was still cooking but there were only four men to cook for. She could do it with her hands tied.

Matt was outside working, so she was too.

She was getting pretty good at riding Maisie now. She could round up the mobs of sheep with him, listening to his plans for building his bloodlines, or explaining how this ewe had triplets last lambing and all of them survived, or introducing her to Roger the Ram, whose bloodlines were suspect but who'd been having his way with the ladies for so long that he didn't have it in him to get rid of him.

His pride in his land and his flock was contagious. Penny found herself starting to decipher individual differences, knowing what to look for in the best breeding stock, looking at the signs of capeweed in the top paddock and frowning because Matt had told her the effort it was to keep the pasture lush and healthy.

Then they started drenching, and working in the house disappeared from her agenda. They lived on soup and sandwiches because Penny was out there, learning how to deal with a drenching gun to make sure the sheep would be pest-free, learning how to encourage the dogs and herd a mob of sheep into the yards, how to be a useful farmhand.

She came in at night tired and filthy—she smelled the same as Samson—and every night she fell into bed exhausted.

She fell into bed with Matt.

On the night of the picnic he'd taken her to his bed and she'd melted into his arms with joy. It felt right. It felt like home.

It was as if she hadn't lived until now. He smiled and her heart sang. He touched her and her body melted into his.

This wasn't forever. She was sensible enough to know those demons were still out there. She was still Matt's housekeeper, being paid the exorbitant wage she'd demanded. He was still her boss.

But he wasn't her boss at night and the nights were theirs. Their nights were a time for no promises, no thought of the future and no looking back on the past.

Here, in Matt's arms, she could pretend the rest

of the world didn't exist. She could forget her father's scorn, Brett's betrayal, her mother's needs.

Here she could pretend she was loved and, for the moment, it was all she asked.

And as for Matt's demons? She wasn't asking questions and neither was he. For both of them the future seemed too far away, too hard. There was just the oasis of now.

Old resolutions were put aside. She knew they were still there—for both of them—but for now why ask questions? Right now was perfect.

If this was all there was, she'd take it.

So would Matt, but in the dawn light he was awake, staring at the ceiling, seeing trouble.

There'd been a couple of phone calls from Darrilyn, hysterical ones—calls that reminded him of times past.

'She's impossible!' Darrilyn had practically screeched it down the phone. 'She's a thirteen-year-old witch. Ray's starting to say he won't have her in the house. All she does is sulk and listen to her appalling music and throw insults at Ray. If it gets any worse… You'll have to cope.'

You'll have to cope.

His mother had used that line. He remembered her getting ready to go out for an evening with her latest boyfriend. He must have been about seven.

'You're a big boy now, Matt. There are cold sausages in the fridge and cola. If I'm not back by morning you know where your school uniform is. Make sure you brush your hair before you walk to school. And make sure you're not late or I'll have teachers asking questions.'

'I don't like being by myself.' He could still hear his childish plea.

'Nonsense,' she'd said. 'Don't be stupid, Matt. I'm entitled to have fun. You'll just have to cope.'

He did have to cope. Somehow.

But this woman in his arms? This woman who trusted absolutely? Penny, who wore her heart on her sleeve...

She was the best thing to happen to him, he thought. She was someone he'd never thought he could meet.

He was a loner. He'd learned not to need anyone. But he lay with her in his arms and he thought it'd be okay. He could love her.

His life was changing. His life right now was better than okay.

But Penny looked at him with love and a voice inside his head was telling him that love came with strings.

If she needed him... If he admitted he needed her...

What was wrong with that?

Nothing, he told himself as she woke and he held her close. As her body melted into his, as the dawn dissolved in a mist of love and desire, the problems of the past seemed far away.

What was wrong with needing this woman?

Nothing at all?

They were at the end of drenching—squirting stuff on the sheep's backs that'd protect them from internal parasites. Penny was having more fun than she'd ever had in her life.

There'd been a mishap. A tree had fallen over a fence. It meant one mob of sheep already drenched had surged through and mingled with the final mob. So Penny was now in charge of drafting.

The sheep were being herded into the yards by the dogs—with Samson helping a lot! Penny stood at the gate separating the runs.

She had to hold the gate, check the markings and direct the sheep either way by opening and shutting the gate.

Ron and Harv stood beyond her in the drenching run, and Matt stood beyond that, doing a fast visual check of each animal. It meant that not only were they drenched but any problems left from the shear, nicks and cuts that hadn't been picked up and hadn't healed, were picked up there and then.

She was part of a team. The sun was warm on her face. Samson was having the time of his life, and so was she.

In an hour or so the final drenching would be

done. She and Matt would head to the house and clean up, and the evening would be theirs.

She felt like singing—though maybe not, she thought. Her nice, calm sheep might decide not to be so calm.

'What's funny?' Matt asked and she glanced along the run and saw him watching her. She smiled at him and he smiled back, and Harv groaned.

'Leave it off, you two. You're enough to curdle milk.' But he was grinning as he said it.

Matt and Penny. The men were starting to treat them like a couple.

It felt…okay.

'I was just considering a little singing to work by,' Penny said with as much dignity as she could muster. 'Like sea shanties. Heave, ho, blow the sheep down.'

'You'd have the sheep scattering into the middle of next week,' Ron told her but he was grinning too, and Penny felt so happy that even a sea shanty wasn't going to cut it.

In deference to the sheep she was singing inside herself, but still she was singing.

She glanced back at Matt again and saw his smile which was a mixture of laughter and pride and something else.

Something that took her breath away.

And then his phone rang. The moment was broken.

Interruptions happened often enough to be mundane. The line slowed. Harv continued with the drenching and Ron moved to do the checking. Penny slowed letting the sheep through. The team worked on, but Matt disappeared behind the shed to talk in private.

And when he returned…he didn't say anything. Work continued, but Penny saw his face and knew that things had changed.

With the drenching finished, Matt excused himself and took Nugget up to the top paddocks to check the flocks. He did it every night, but tonight he took longer and went alone. 'I need some time to think,' he told Penny and she headed inside feeling worried.

She showered and changed, made dinner, waited and eventually ate hers and put Matt's in the warming drawer.

She sat on the veranda as she always did, but tonight she sat with a sense of foreboding.

She'd seen Matt's face when he'd returned from the call. She knew trouble when she saw it.

She knew this man by now.

Finally he came. He snagged himself a beer, brought his plate from the warming drawer and came out to join her.

'All's well,' he said briefly.

She didn't comment. She knew a lie when she heard one.

She hugged Samson while he ate. She'd washed him while she was waiting and he was fluffy and clean on her knee. He looked almost normal, a little white poodle instead of a sheepdog.

And with that word *normal* came another thought. What was normal?

Her life before, where Samson was clean all the time?

Life before Matt.

'That was great,' Matt said, and Penny looked at his empty plate and knew something was seriously wrong.

'Sausages and chips that have been in the warming drawer for over an hour? I don't think so.'

'Your cooking's always great.' He shrugged and tried to smile. 'You're great.'

'What's wrong?'

He didn't answer. He hadn't come to the edge of the veranda to join her as he usually did. He was sitting on the cane sofa, back in the shadows.

The silence stretched. It felt as if something was hovering above their heads, Penny thought.

Something fearful?

'Matt?' she said again, and it was a question.

He rose and walked to the edge of the veranda. For a couple of moments he stayed silent, staring out into the night. Finally he spoke.

'Penny, Lily's coming.'

Lily? His daughter.

'That's good? Isn't it?'

'The timing's appalling, but it is.'

'Why is the timing appalling?'

'I never thought she'd come so soon.' He hesitated. 'To be honest, I never thought she'd come at all.'

'So why now?'

'The phone call this afternoon was from Darrilyn. It seems there was a fight last night between Lily and Darrilyn's boyfriend. Apparently Ray's a hunter. He has trophies all over the house. He's just been to Africa and brought home stuffed heads from his latest kill, and it seems Lily hit the roof. According to Darrilyn, she said some unforgivable things and Ray hit her. They went out and left Lily at home, and Lily took scissors and Ray's razor and shaved every single stuffed head in the house.'

'Oh…' Penny almost laughed. So the kid had spunk. 'Oh, my…'

'So Ray wants her gone, now. She's been in boarding school, but it's vacation and Ray says she's not even staying with him until school starts. And Darrilyn… To be honest, I don't think she ever really wanted her. Having Lily's simply been a way of accessing my money and now it's all too hard. So Darrilyn's organizing a school here but, until she can start, she's sending her to me. She's putting her on a plane as we speak. I'll pick her up in Adelaide and bring her here. Not for long, though. Darrilyn's currently researching schools, probably finding the most expensive one she can make me pay for.'

'I…see.' She felt vaguely ill for the unknown and unwanted Lily. Maybe she could help, she thought.

And then she thought: *No—really no.*

Because suddenly she saw exactly what the problem was and, looking at Matt's shadowed face, she knew that he'd got there too. She understood the heaviness.

She was suddenly imagining the thoughts of the unknown Lily. The kid was being thrown out of the only home she knew and was heading halfway across the world to meet a father she saw twice a year.

She'd be terrified.

But Matt would have told his daughter about this farm. All her life she'd have heard stories of Jindalee, of Ron and Harv and Donald, and the dogs and the sheep. Maybe she knew about Maisie as well. Being here… Riding Maisie… Exploring the farm with her father…finally they might bond.

But, to do that, to have any chance at all, they couldn't have an outsider, a pink princess tagging along with them.

She saw the whole situation now, and it made her feel…hollow? Lily would arrive traumatised—

Penny knew enough of troubled teenagers to re-
alise that. She'd need all Matt's attention and more.

But, as for Penny? As for Penny and Matt? Well,
that was never going to work out.

Relationships and Penny? *Ha*.

And reality flooded back. For these last few
nights, lying with Matt's body curved protectively
against hers, she'd allowed herself to dream, but
that was all it was. A dream. Matt had needed her
over shearing, and he'd enjoyed her in his bed. But
now he no longer needed her and it was time to
move on.

Matt knew it. They both did. So say it.

'I need to go.'

'No.' Matt's response was a savage growl, but
she met his gaze and she knew he saw the situation as clearly as she did.

He should be joyful that his daughter was finally
arriving. Instead he was heavy-hearted because an
embryonic relationship was getting in the way of
what had to happen.

Matt Fraser was a good man. An honourable
man. She knew he'd do the right thing, but for now
the right thing was to put his daughter first.

So if he couldn't—maybe she had to be cruel
for him.

'It's been fun,' she managed and she set Samson down and pulled herself to her feet. 'But you

don't need me here when Lily arrives. She'll need your sole attention.'

'I want you to stay.'

'Do you really?' She put her hands on her hips, feeling a surge of anger. She'd faced enough harsh reality in relationships to be used to confronting the truth, and he needed to see it, too. Coating it with sugar, with regrets, with apologies, didn't help at all. 'Matt, I came uninvited. I've had a wonderful time and, what's more, you've paid me brilliantly. It's been the job of a lifetime and you and I have had fun. But it's time for Samson and me to move on.'

'Penny, I need you to stay.'

But the anger was still with her. She knew impossibility when she saw it.

'Why?'

'Because I think I might love you.'

And the night stopped, just like that.

Love.

It was a tiny word. It was a word that was terrifying.

Normal people understood the love thing, she thought bleakly. Normal parents picked their kids up when they fell over, kissed scraped knees, told them they were loved and set them down to toddle off to the next scrape.

For Penny, though… *'Penny, how can you expect us to love you if you look a disgrace? Why aren't you more like your sister? For heaven's sake, lose a few pounds—that a daughter of mine looks pudgy... If you love us, girl, you'll do what I tell you...'*

It was always her father's voice, with her mother in the background, looking distressed but saying nothing.

And then Brett... *'Penny, I love you and all I want is to make you happy.'*

Love. It should make her heart sing and yet all it did was make her mistrust.

'No,' she said, more harshly than she intended. She hauled her dignity around her like a cloak, and maybe only she could see how tattered that cloak was. 'Love. It doesn't mean anything. We've known each other for how long? To talk of love is crazy. We need to face reality. These last weeks have been great but you don't need me any more. If and when Lily settles into school and you'd like to catch up then maybe we can meet, but let's leave it with no promises. Don't make your life any more complicated than it already is. Samson and I will leave in the morning.'

'What will you do?' And he'd accepted it, she thought. He knew there was no choice.

He really did love his daughter and he was an honourable man.

'I'll go back to Sydney,' she told him. 'I'll get myself together and decide on a serious career path

rather than head back to the outback on a whim.
I might even help my mother face this wedding
down.'

'Penny, don't!'

'I think I must,' she said, striving for lightness.
'Because I love my mum. Like you love Lily. We
shouldn't fight these things even if we want to. You
know your first commitment needs to be to Lily?'

'Yes,' he growled. 'But I don't have to like it.'

But she smiled and shook her head. 'This is your
daughter and I'm very sure you do. Love between
you and me? Well, that's something we can control. It's something we can back away from because
we both know it won't work. But the way you love
Lily, and the way I love my mum, well, that's non-
negotiable.'

And then she couldn't help herself. She stood
on tiptoe and kissed him lightly on the lips, but retreated before he had the chance to respond.

'You're a wonderful man, Matt Fraser,' she told
him. 'I've had an amazing time. You've rescued
me really well, but now it's time for your rescued
maiden to move on.'

Matt stayed on the veranda for a long time.

She was desperately hurt. He could see it in the
way her face had closed, in the way she'd tucked
herself into herself, in the dignity she'd summoned
as she'd said goodnight.

All he wanted to do was follow her, fold her into his arms and tell her how loved she was. How she was the best thing to happen to him…ever? Love was something they could control? *Ha!*

But he'd known her for less than a month. Maybe she had it right.

He thought of his mother, bursting in the door after a night out. *'Darling, I've met the most wonderful man.'* Then there'd be weeks, even months, of glowing happiness while she ignored everything else but the new love in her life. In the end Matt had learned to ignore it, put his head down, battle through as best he could until his mother finally surfaced. Even when he was tiny, she'd wanted him to pick up the pieces.

'Oh, darling, give your mummy a hug. Hug her until she feels better. Is there anything in the fridge? Oh, sweetheart, is that all? You need to come with me to the Welfare. They'll give me more if I take you with me.'

This wasn't anything like that, he thought savagely. It didn't come close.

But his daughter? Lily had been brought up with Darrilyn's version of the same scenario. Darrilyn had moved from one disastrous situation to another as she'd searched for the next socially desirable catch. If he'd thought there was any way he could help he'd have moved to the States, but Darrilyn had sole custody, granted by the US courts.

His visits had been formally arranged and necessarily brief. But now, finally, Lily was coming home.

He'd always told her she was welcome here. 'If ever your mother agrees, you have a home in Australia,' he'd told her. 'A farm, your own horse, stability. And a dad who loves you and only you.'

Okay, it had been a promise that in retrospect was stupid, but he'd never believed he could fall for another woman.

He had fallen, but what he had with Penny was only weeks old. Even his mother's relationships had looked rosy after less than a month.

'Leave it,' he told himself heavily and he knew he couldn't do anything else. He'd try and talk to Penny again at breakfast. Try and explain.

Except she understood. He knew she did.

She got it.

She was one amazing woman. When Lily was settled, he could find her…

'Yeah? You think she'll hang around and wait?'

There was no answer. She'd gone to bed. Even the dogs had gone to bed.

He was alone, as he'd promised his daughter he would be.

'And that's the way it has to be.' He knew it but he didn't have to like it.

He'd hurt Penny but how could he fix it?

'Maybe in time…'

Or not. *Leave it,* he told himself. For now he had this one chance with his daughter and he couldn't blow it.

Even if the hurt in Penny's eyes was like a stab to his own heart.

CHAPTER TEN

MALLEY'S DIDN'T WANT HER, or if they did she didn't stick around to find out. Malley's was too close to Jindalee. Too close to Matt.

She headed back to Sydney because her mother's pleas were still ringing in her ears. She no longer had an excuse not to attend her sister's wedding and, for some strange reason, she now felt she had the strength to be there.

She wasn't sure where it had come from but this new strength was with her. The new, improved Penny... She could have cried all the way home, but she refused. Instead she lowered the sunroof, put every powerful woman singer she knew on her sound system and let them rip. *I am woman*... She surely was. She arrived back in Sydney sunburned and with no voice but she didn't care.

Anger helped. And a new-found determination.

She'd put her career aside once because she loved her mother. What a disaster. Then she'd thought she'd loved Brett and where had that got her?

Now...she'd exposed her heart even more, and all she felt was pain.

'So no one needs me and I refuse to need anyone,' she told Samson. 'Who needs love?' It didn't quite work but it was worth a try.

Her mother was overjoyed to see her but Penny didn't stay at home except to sleep. She had things to do. Moping gave her time to think and the last thing she wanted was thinking time.

In some strange way things had changed inside her. She thought of the times she'd pleaded with her father to do what she wanted, and had passively accepted dismissal and scorn. But this time…

'I'm setting up my own catering company,' she told her parents. 'My plan is to do proper meals— family meals. If a young mum has a baby, I'll come in with a full week's worth of nutritious comfort food. If someone's ill, I'll supply what the family needs. I'll start small, but I'm thinking in the end I'll have staff and a fleet of delivery vans and caterers who can move into people's homes. And I'll be hands-on. Any time there's a need for a good feed, I'm your girl.'

'I won't have the media saying my daughter's a servant,' her father snapped but she'd had enough.

'I'm not a servant, and the only time I've ever felt like one was when I tried to please you. Look where that got me. So this time I'm pleasing myself and don't you dare put pressure on Mum to make me change my mind. And I won't be staying in Sydney. I'll be moving to Adelaide or Melbourne. It depends where I can get decent premises and that'll take time but I'll do it right. And Mum,

I won't let Dad blackmail me into doing what he wants by using your sadness, so you might as well get used to the new order.'

She left them speechless. To say her father was unused to the women in his family standing up to him would be an understatement but she'd done it. She'd stay for a few weeks. She'd get her mother through this wedding, she'd get her own head together and then move on.

Matt would be proud, she thought, but that was a concept that hurt. So, instead of thinking about Matt, she forced herself to focus on work.

She put out feelers for long-term premises in Melbourne and Adelaide but she was sensible enough to accept that long-term plans should be put on hold until she was emotionally level-headed again.

She found a decent commercial kitchen and took a short-term lease, then contacted a local refuge for the homeless. The homeless were delighted, and cooking was a balm.

She needed someone to help her if she was going to do the deliveries as well so she advertised for an assistant. A young woman applied who was from Adelaide. Was that a sign? Maybe her new life could be in Adelaide.

It was too soon to decide. For now she was busy. She was doing what she wanted.

So why did she feel so empty?

At least Matt had banished the humiliation Felicity and Brett had caused, she conceded. That was the one good thing, so when her mother asked again—very tentatively—about the family pre-wedding dinner, she agreed.

Do it and move on, she told herself. *I am woman...*

'That's lovely, dear,' Louise said. 'It'll be just the five of us.'

Just like last time, Penny thought, and was proud of herself for not saying it.

So, two weeks after she'd left Jindalee, five days before her sister's wedding, she found herself dressing up and heading downstairs for a formal pre-wedding dinner.

Not a dinner cooked by her, though. Her parents had hired a trendy caterer for the occasion.

'It'll be something with kale in it,' she muttered to herself. 'With accents of Japanese on the side. Seaweed maybe.'

She thought suddenly of her shearers being given kale and seaweed and found herself grinning.

'Hold that thought,' she muttered and headed for the dining room. She was halfway down the grand staircase when the doorbell rang.

Felicity and Brett had arrived together ten minutes earlier. She could hear Brett pontificating with her father in the dining room. They weren't expecting anyone else.

Her parents' butler swung the door wide. The porch was well lit.

It was Matt.

She was halfway down the stairs and she was dressed as he'd never seen her—in a sky-blue cocktail dress that accentuated her curves to perfection. It had a mandarin collar, slit deep to reveal the beautiful curves of her breasts. It had tiny capped sleeves, a cinched waist and a skirt that swirled softly to below her knees. She was wearing high silver stilettoes and loopy silver earrings. Her hair was caught up in a soft knot of tumbled curls.

She looked elegant and poised and about a million miles from the Penny he knew. She looked as if she belonged here.

What was he doing? He felt like he should cut and run.

But it had cost him considerable trouble to get this far. There were security gates at the start of the mansion's long drive but by coincidence they'd been left open. That coincidence had taken research, an extensive phone call to the family butler, an explanation he was hardly ready to give and an eye-watering bank transfer.

So now he was where he needed to be, but did Penny want him? This house was all marble stucco, Grecian columns—grand, grand and more grand. And Penny looked…amazing.

Was this the Penny he knew?

He'd spent the last two weeks fighting an internal battle, which he'd lost. He was in Sydney, Penny was close and he knew her appalling family dinner was tonight. Letting her face it by herself seemed the act of a coward.

That was what he'd told himself, but he knew it was more than that. He'd spent two weeks without her and those two weeks had left him feeling gutted.

It was too late to back out now. Penny had seen him. She paused on the stairway, looking stunned. 'Matt,' she breathed and he felt his world settle a little. Just to hear her voice made him feel better.

'Hi.' He smiled, but the butler moved imperceptibly, blocking the path between them. Refusing him entry.

Fair enough. The man had agreed to let him as far as the door. He now had to resume his role.

'I had no right to come,' he managed, talking up towards Penny. 'But I don't have your phone details. I've brought Lily to Sydney to her new school and I wanted…well, I hoped for your advice.' He took a deep breath and looked again at the vision in blue. *Wow.*

'I'd hoped to talk to you,' he managed. 'But if it's a bad time…'

'What's happening?'

A woman emerged from double doors leading

from the hall. She was slim and elegant, immaculately groomed, looking worried. Penny's mother?

'Brian, who is it?' she demanded of the butler. 'You know George said no interruptions. Felicity says Brett must have failed to hit the remote and left the gate open. George is already angry.'

Matt glanced again at Penny. Penny's initial smile had faded. She was standing like stone.

Okay, back to the plan. He turned to her mother. 'I'm sorry to interrupt,' he said. 'I met Penny when she was working in South Australia. I've brought my daughter to school in Sydney but I didn't have Penny's contact details. Your number's not listed but I knew where you live. I'd like to talk to her for a moment, but if I'm intruding…'

'Are you her friend?' The woman's gaze flashed to her daughter, interest quickening. 'I *knew* she'd met someone.'

'Mum, no…'

But welcoming good-looking men into her orbit was one of Louise's principal skills, coming to the fore no matter what personal turmoil surrounded her. 'Come in. Brian, let the man in. Penny, introduce us.'

'This…this is Matt,' Penny stammered. 'He's a farmer…from where I worked. Matt, this is my mother, Louise.'

'A farmer?' Louise's smile hit high beam. 'How lovely. Come and have dinner with us.'

And this was exactly what he'd hoped for. Plan B was to sweep her up and take her out to dinner somewhere else. Or leave.

But a third option seemed most likely. 'He can't stay,' Penny said in a haunted voice and her mother looked at her again. Harder.

'Really? You don't want him to?'

He'd accept it. His plan had been simply to give her an escape route, or support, or both, but only if she wanted it. If she didn't then he'd walk away.

But Louise was looking exasperated. She turned back to him. 'Dear, if you know Penny then you'll know this is an awkward night for her,' she confided. 'She's agreed to have dinner with her sister and her ex-fiancé. Has she told you about it?'

'I…yes.'

'Then what we want,' she said with asperity, 'is a stranger to leaven the occasion.' She eyed him up and down. It'd have been too obvious to arrive dressed for a dinner party, but he was wearing new chinos, a decent shirt and a tie. His jacket was aged leather but it was decent quality. He could see Louise assessing and deciding to approve.

'Please, come on in,' she told him. 'Penny, you want him to stay? Don't you?'

Did she want him to stay?

Yes! part of her was yelling, but this was a new Penny. Okay, she'd only had two weeks of wearing her new skin but it had been a long drive back to Sydney and she'd had that radio up loud.

I am woman...

She was not her mother. She was not a doormat.

Did Matt want something? Didn't they all? She was suddenly feeling unbearably tired.

But her mother was letting her guard slip. Her social façade had disappeared and she was addressing her daughter with a degree of desperation. 'Penny, agree,' she told her. 'What your father is asking of you is impossible.' She turned back to Matt. 'Penny's ex-fiancé and her pregnant sister are here, and her father's expecting her to act as if everything's normal. I know she can do it—my daughter can do anything—but your presence...' She turned back to Penny again. 'Sweetheart, it would help. You know it would.'

It was the first time her mother had acknowledged her pain, and her words pierced a chink into the armour she'd so carefully built.

And then Matt looked up and met her gaze. He didn't smile. His gaze was serious, steady—loving?

And the chink grew wider.

'I won't be where I'm not wanted,' he said simply. 'Penny, if you'd like me to stay, then of course I will. You helped me and of course I'd like to help you. But I didn't come to intrude.'

Of course I'd like to help you. How could she believe that?

And then she thought: *I told him the date of this dinner.* Was it possible he'd planned this?

The thought that he'd do that for her... It was like a lightning bolt.

He'd come...for her.

'Stay.' She couldn't believe she'd said it, but it was out there.

His gaze didn't leave hers.

'You're sure?'

'Yes.' And she was sure. He'd planned it. It would be too big a coincidence. She gazed at Brian, who was looking blandly at nothing. Matt. Brian.

This was a plot!

For her.

'Then thank you, I will,' he said but still he didn't smile.

Her mother did, though. This was what she was all about—trying to please everyone, keeping her family happy. And Penny had a man! Penny could almost hear her think it, and the fact that he looked...well, he looked a hunk, did him no disservice in her mother's eyes.

Her father, though... And Brett and Felicity? A complicated night had suddenly become a whole lot more complicated.

But he'd planned it. For her.

Introductions all around.

George was urbane enough to be polite, even

though he clearly didn't like his family dinner being gate-crashed.

'Sherry?' he asked Matt. 'It's a magnificent one my people have sourced from Almacenista. Or would you prefer a red? We have an aged...'

'I'd like a beer, if you have one,' Matt told him. 'Otherwise, water's fine.'

'As you wish,' George said stiffly, glancing at Penny as if she was responsible for allowing the cat to drag something in. And, as Brian poured a designer beer, he homed right in. 'So... Matthew, is it? What do you do?'

'I run sheep on the Murray,' Matt told him.

'You're a farmer?'

'Yes, sir.'

'That's where my daughter met you?'

'It is.'

'Her mother tells me it's flood country. How long have you been there?'

'Ten years.'

'It's a family farm?'

'No, sir, I bought it.'

'Well, that's a risk I wouldn't have taken. Small holdings take a lot to make them pay and if they're on flood plains...' Matt had clearly been pigeon-holed and dismissed. 'I wish you well making a success of it.'

'Thank you,' Matt said. He took a swig of his beer and Penny almost smiled. Matt was drinking from the finest crystal but he drank like he was swigging from a can. She saw the exact moment when he stopped holding himself erect, when his voice took on the country drawl he used among the men—when he decided that if George had him down as a small time farmer then that was what he'd be.

And he'd also decided to be jovial.

'So Brett,' Matt said to Penny's ex-fiancé as he finished his beer and Brian poured him another. 'What do you do?'

'I'm a financial controller for the Hindmarsh-Firth Corporation,' Brett told him. 'If you understand what that is. Imagine the day-to-day cash flow problems you have on the farm and multiply them by thousands. Possibly millions.' Brett was smirking a little. He hadn't realised yet, Penny thought, that Matt's arrival had made him look small.

And then she thought, why hadn't *she* realised how small Brett was? Or maybe the word shouldn't be small. Maybe the word should be *insignificant*.

'Well, that must be fascinating,' Matt was saying, his voice full of awareness of the huge responsibility Brett faced. 'All that adding up. So…you work for your fiancée's father?'

'He works *with* my father,' Felicity snapped.

'Of course. And you, Felicity?' His attention was suddenly switched to high beam on Penny's half-sister. 'Penny tells me you've been overseas. Working or pleasure?'

Felicity was not in a great mood. She was twelve weeks pregnant and she was nauseous. She was drinking soda, which she hated. What was worse, the new dress she'd bought specifically for this event only ten days ago would no longer fit, but she wasn't pregnant enough for the sexy maternity clothes she'd been admiring when she'd decided to try for a baby. She'd had to revert to last year's fashion.

And now her half-sister was sitting opposite her with a guy who might well be a small time farmer but wow...

'It's nice that Penny's found herself a friend,' Felicity said waspishly, ignoring Matt's question. 'Even if she had to go halfway across Australia to do it.'

'And wasn't I lucky that she did?' Matt said, and he smiled at Penny, and that smile...it even made her mother gasp. 'I hear you found your man much closer to home. Not that I'd describe myself as Penny's man, but I hope I'm her friend. That's such a privilege I can't begin to tell you.' He glanced at Brett. 'The local men obviously don't know what they're missing. Penny's one in a million.'

And suddenly, despite her discomfiture, Penny started enjoying herself. Matt could hold his own. Her mother was beaming. But the rest...

Her father and Brett were reacting like two roosters with a much larger and more impressive rooster invading their patch. Both were assured of their own superiority but Matt's calm acceptance of snide criticism had unnerved them.

And Felicity was jealous. Again.

Penny watched Matt smile at something her mother said. She witnessed his skill in deflecting Brett's barbs, and she watched him flirt mildly with the bristling Felicity. He was placating her with compliments. He was also exposing her shallowness and making Brett angry, but she knew instinctively that he was doing it only because he was angry on her behalf.

He'd come tonight, to this dinner, because he'd thought she needed him. She did need him.

No! Had she learned nothing? She did not need him! *I am woman...*

I'm no longer the poor relation at this table, she thought. She had her embryo catering company. She'd stood up to her father. She'd baked—successfully—for a full mob of shearers, and she had a friend. And such a friend.

She looked across the table at Matt and found him watching her, and suddenly she was smiling and smiling.

'How long are you in Sydney?'

'I've been here for a week and I may stay longer,' he told her. 'I need to wait until I'm sure Lily's settled.'

'What school's she going to?'

Matt told her—and that pretty much brought the conversation to a standstill.

'Why…that's the one Penelope and Felicity attended,' Louise gasped.

'How can you afford that?' George demanded and Penny thought a lesser man might have got up and punched her father's lights out for the offensiveness in the way he'd barked it.

But Matt merely shrugged. 'I'm divorced,' he said neutrally. 'My ex-wife has money.'

'Lucky for some,' Brett sneered but Penny wasn't listening. She was side-tracked.

'Matt, I hated that school.'

'It's the one Darrilyn's chosen.'

'Then un-choose it.'

'I'd like to talk to you about it, if I could,' he confessed. 'But now's not the time.'

And then the main course arrived, with all the theatre the hired, trendy catering staff could muster. Penny fell silent.

The choice of Matt's daughter's school was nothing to do with her, she told herself. It was none of her business.

But Matt wanted her advice.

He wanted her to be his friend.

He'd come tonight to help her.

The talk went on around her. She was aware that Matt was watching her but she wouldn't meet his gaze.

He chatted on easily, ignoring the undercurrents, making the gathering seem almost civil, but Penny's mother also fell silent. She looked as if cogs were whirring unseen. Comments to Louise went unanswered, and then, halfway through the dessert, she looked up from her peach flambé and beamed.

Penny knew that beam. *Uh oh.*

'Matthew?' Louise asked and Penny thought *uh oh, uh, oh, uh oh.*

'Ma'am?'

'What are you doing on Saturday?'

'I'm not sure,' he told her, glancing at a bemused Penny. 'It depends on my daughter.'

'Bring her to Felicity and Brett's wedding,' Louise said, with what was, for her, a defiant look at her husband. 'We seem to have invited half of Australian's *Who's Who* to this wedding so two more won't make a spot of difference. Do you have a suit?'

'I do,' he said gravely.

'Then I'd like to invite you. Please,' she added. 'If you're a friend of Penny's then you'll know that there are things about this wedding that make her… uncomfortable. You'll be doing us all a favour if you come. We'd love it if you could bring your daughter, but for the night…' She cast an uncertain glance at Penny but decided to forge right on. 'Come as Penny's partner. Like a little family. It'll take the media attention off Penny and I'm sure we'd all be very grateful.'

There was a deathly silence.

George and Brett and Felicity all looked as if Matt would be doing them the very opposite of a favour.

Louise smiled defiantly on.

And Matt looked at Penny.

'Penny?'

Matt, as her partner, at a wedding she didn't wish to go near?

But this was her half-sister's wedding and, hate it as she did, she'd made the decision to support her mother. The media fuss if she didn't go would be worse than if she did.

And, besides, there were parts of tonight's dinner she'd actually enjoyed.

Matt.

In a suit.

With his daughter?

His daughter was being sent to a school she'd surely hate.

Okay, she didn't want to be involved but she was. Like it or not. But she wouldn't be a doormat.

'I'm setting up a catering company,' she told him. 'I have temporary premises in Darling Harbour and I'll be there all day tomorrow. If you'd like to come around we can discuss it then.' And she could tell him exactly what she thought of his choice of school.

'I'd appreciate that,' he said gravely.

'So you will come to the wedding?' Louise demanded.

'Only if Penny wants me to,' Matt told her. 'I'd never pressure her.'

But it was too much for Felicity. She'd been growing angrier and angrier.

'Penny doesn't choose the guests,' she said in a voice that dripped ice. 'This is my wedding. I decide.'

'It's my wedding too,' Brett corrected her. '*Our* wedding, sweetheart. But he's certainly not on my list.'

But Felicity didn't take rebukes well. From anyone. She cast her fiancé a look loaded with such acid it could have cleaned warts off toads, and of course she changed her mind. 'Oh, for heaven's sake,' she muttered. 'If it'll make Penny feel better then of course she can bring a friend.' And she sent Penny such a condescending smile that she thought she might throw up.

'I don't need your sympathy,' she managed.

'But you have it,' Felicity said and smirked. 'Brett's in love with me.'

'Of course he is.' But then Penny hesitated. She cast a look at Matt. He was just…here. Big and strong and solid. She had backup, she thought. He'd come to support her—why not use it? Why not say what she'd been wanting to say to a big sister she'd once looked up to? 'But Felicity, have you any idea what you're getting into?' she asked gently. 'Brett went behind my back to get you pregnant. Do you think he'll stay loyal to you? You'll have family support, no matter what you do. It's not too late to pull out of a wedding you're not committed to.'

And that was too much for her father.

'Keep out of what's not your business,' George snarled. 'The wedding's happening in five days.'

'And this man's not coming,' Brett snapped.

'I agree,' George snapped back. 'My wife's in charge of the invitation list for this side of the family, and this man's not on it.'

So that was it.

Except Matt was looking at Louise.

Just looking.

And suddenly Penny wasn't sure what was happening.

Matt had charisma. Or something? She wasn't sure what. She only knew that Matt was looking directly at her mother and whatever was passing between them had the power to make the rest of the table shut up.

Even her father seemed momentarily baffled. Stymied by silence.

When finally Matt spoke his voice was low, reasonable and total mesmerizing.

'It seems to me,' he said softly, speaking directly to Louise and no one else, 'that Penny's been treated appallingly by those who love her. It seems to me that no one's spoken up for her. She's attending her sister's wedding—to support you, I suspect—and in the circumstances that leaves me stunned. If she needs me to lend her even more dignity and honour—two virtues that Penny already has in spades—then it would be my very real pleasure to be there for her. But, ma'am, I suspect that decision is up to you. And maybe it's time we all showed Penny how much she means to us. Especially, maybe, it's time her mother did.'

And he smiled at Louise, a smile that took Penny's breath away. A smile she'd never seen before.

'Maybe it's the right time now,' he said gently. 'To show Penny how much she's loved by us all.'

Silence. Deathly silence.

George was staring at Matt as if he were something from another planet.

Felicity and Brett were sitting with their mouths open, obviously struggling to find the words to retaliate.

But Penny's mother stared at Matt and he kept smiling at her. She stared...and then she turned to Penny.

'Penny,' she whispered and Penny gave her a wobbly smile.

'It's okay, Mum.'

'But it's not,' Louise whispered and she looked again at Matt.

And then, suddenly, Louise was standing. Her eyes were over-bright. She'd had one, possibly two more wines than was wise, but her speech was clear. 'Matt's right,' she quavered, speaking to Felicity. 'I've done every scrap of organization for this wedding, and you and your father haven't lifted a finger. And after the way you've treated *my* daughter...I could make one phone call to the caterers tomorrow, and with the demand for their services you'd find yourself without a wedding. Even if you did manage to salvage it, the ensuing media fuss would cause a riot.'

'You wouldn't,' George barked. 'Felicity's your daughter. We agreed when we married that you'd...'

'Look after her as if she were my own? Yes, I did.' She glanced again at Matt and what she saw there seemed to give her courage. 'I've loved Felicity even though she has a perfectly good mother of her own. But I've had enough. Felicity's not acting like my daughter. She and Brett have hurt Penny deeply, so deeply that all deals are off.'

And she turned again and looked at Matt.

Penny thought, *It's as if Matt's giving her*

strength. She'd never known her mother to stand up for herself. Or stand up for her.

What was it about Matt?

'I've shut up for years,' Louise went on, enunciating every syllable with care. 'But now… Felicity, Penny's right to question what you're doing. You took Brett because Penny was marrying him and you were jealous of the attention. Amazing bridal gowns and maternity clothes are the latest fashion. Penny was getting what you don't have, and you've always thought like that. So now you're having your wedding and you're having your baby and you have Brett. And if you don't let Penny have Matt…'

'I don't want Matt,' Penny managed and the look Louise cast her was wild.

'It doesn't matter,' she told her. 'He's lovely— even I can see that. But it's *your* choice. Matt said it himself.'

'It is your choice,' Matt said. The corners of his mouth were twitching. The table seemed in total shock. 'But Penny, we're talking about a partner for a wedding, not a choice of life partner. Louise, thank you for your kind invitation. I may well take you up on it, if Penny thinks it's appropriate.' He smiled at Penny, a reassuring smile that held warmth and strength and promise but then he rose. 'I need to go,' he told her apologetically. 'I'm expecting a call from New York in half an hour. But are you okay by yourself here?' He cast a glance at the almost apoplectic George. 'There's room at the Caledonian. You can come back with me if you like.' And then he looked at Louise. 'Your mum too, if she'd like.'

If she'd like, Penny thought wildly. To get up from this table and run...

No.

I am woman?

Her world was quaking, but running away wasn't an answer. And running to Matt? For protection? For sympathy?

She had no need of either, she thought, and she looked at her father.

How had he grown to be such an ogre when he was just a puffed-up bully?

She looked at her mum and she grinned.

'We can look after ourselves, can't we, Mum?'

Louise was wavering a little on her feet—she really had had too much wine—but once again she looked at Matt and what she saw there seemed to reassure her.

'I...yes. I believe we can.'

'Excellent,' Penny said. She smiled at Matt and only she knew how much of an effort it cost her to stay perky.

'We're fine,' she told Matt. 'Obviously, I'm not sure about the wedding—for all sorts of reasons. But I'll tell you where my catering premises are and if you're still interested then we'll talk about it tomorrow.'

'Tomorrow,' Matt said and smiled at her and her heart twisted in such a way…

Tomorrow.

It was enough.

CHAPTER ELEVEN

PENNY'S NEW ASSISTANT arrived at ten the next morning. Noreen was a shy nineteen-year-old who was practically shaking in her boots. During the phone interview she'd seemed confident and perky, but it had obviously been an act. The only way to settle her and see what she could do was to cook.

And the promise from the interview was more than fulfilled. By late afternoon the kitchen was filled with the smells of tantalizing food.

Penny was covered in flour, elbows deep in baking, trying to focus on what Noreen was doing—and trying very hard not to wonder why Matt hadn't come.

If Noreen hadn't been here she might have gone crazy, she thought, but then she thought she was going a little crazy anyway.

And then the outside bell rang and her heart seemed to stop.

'Do those pies need to come out of the oven?' Noreen asked and her world settled a little. Pies. Cooking. That was the important stuff.

Not Matt?

She wiped her hands on her apron, which made no difference to her general level of messiness.

She ran a floury hand through her curls—*gee, that helped*—and then she tugged the door open.

Matt was right in front of her—and so was his daughter. He was holding her hand.

She looked young for thirteen, but there was no mistaking who she was. She was thin and dark like her father. Too thin. Her hair was shaped into an elfin cut. Her eyes looked too big for her face, and they were shadowed.

She looked like a nervous colt, needing to escape but not sure where to run.

She was wearing the school uniform Penny had loathed and she looked so scared it was all Penny could do not to gather her into her arms. But she'd been thirteen once, and she knew such a thing was unthinkable.

She stood back and smiled a welcome. 'Hi,' she managed. 'I'd started to think you weren't coming.'

'I've been at Lily's school.' He looked almost as nervous as his daughter. 'Penny, this is my daughter, Lily. You don't mind that we came together?'

'Of course not.' She stepped back to let them in. 'Noreen and I are in the middle of baking. We have fifty homeless men to feed tonight. We've just finished apple pies. We're now making gingerbread men, as a post dinner snack.'

'Gingerbread men?' Matt said faintly and Penny fixed him with a look.

'Shearers need calories and so do the homeless,

but the homeless have more time than shearers. So we'll feed them calories and then have fun. We thought we'd ice them with little backpacks and swags. Our aim is to make everyone smile.'

She cast a glance at Lily and saw her gaze around the messy, warm kitchen. She had the same starved look she remembered from her own childhood, when the kitchen was a refuge.

She thought of Matt's story, of this girl standing up to her stepfather, with his appalling stuffed animals, and the chord of recognition grew louder. 'Do you like cooking?'

'I haven't done much,' Lily whispered. She gazed at the bowls of coloured icing and piping bags. 'It looks fun but I wouldn't know what to do.'

But Noreen, herself a gangly adolescent, saw a kindred spirit and beamed.

'It's easy,' she scoffed. 'I'll show you.' So, two minutes later, Noreen and Lily were piping multicoloured skirts on gingerbread ladies and Penny and Matt were free to talk.

Matt couldn't believe the transformation in his daughter. Lily was intent on her piping. Noreen said something to her and she giggled.

Matt felt as if he might cry.

He felt the strain lift from his face as his daughter relaxed.

'So what's happening?' Penny asked him. 'I can't

tell you how grateful I am for last night, but now… You look more tired than when you were facing thousands of sheep and no cook.'

He gave a tired smile. 'Maybe I am,' he said. 'I've had one heck of a day.'

'Want to tell me about it?'

She led him over to the table at the end of the room. Sun was streaming in through the clerestory windows overhead. The room was full of the smells of new baking.

It felt like home, Matt thought, and then he realized he didn't really know what home was. And neither did Lily.

Suddenly there was a mug of tea in front of him and Penny was sitting opposite him. Waiting.

The last thing he wanted was to offload his problems onto her. The last thing he wanted was to need her.

'Tell me,' she said simply.

Penny had driven away from him because he'd put his daughter first. How could he do it again? But he glanced across at Lily and he knew that once again there was no choice.

'I knew there'd be settling in problems with a new school,' he started. 'But I hoped it'd work. But this morning she rang and she couldn't stop crying.'

'Because?'

His gaze was still on Lily. She seemed so young.

Thirteen… He'd hoped she'd be old enough to fend for herself.

She wasn't.

'She's been there for a week,' he told her. 'And she's been put into a shared dorm with three other girls. But it seems they had to give up a settee so they could fit her bed into the room and they resent it. They complained to the school and to their parents, and then they stopped speaking to her. But they still didn't get what they wanted. Lily had to stay. Finally this morning they woke her with iced water tossed in her face. And they gave her a note.'

'A note?'

'It seems they're the school bullies,' he told her. 'Girls with rich families, used to getting their own way. The note told her that she should leave. It said no girl in the school will talk to her and if they do then they'll get the same treatment she does.'

'Oh, Matt…'

'So of course I fronted the headmistress,' he told her. 'I showed her the note and was expecting horror. But instead I heard pretty much what Lily did. "Friendships have been formed, Mr Fraser," she said. "It's difficult to make the girls accept an outsider, especially when she's arriving mid-term."

'Then I asked if Lily could be moved into a friendlier dorm and I had my head bitten off. She can't be bothered with what she terms "childish squabbles". She says if that dorm's unsuitable then the school's unsuitable.'

'So?'

'So we grabbed Lily's gear and moved out,' Matt told her.

'Oh, Matt.' And then she smiled. 'Good for you.'

'Yeah,' he said morosely, still watching his daughter. 'But now… Darrilyn's decreed that's the school she'll attend, and I don't want her taking her back to the States.'

'Does Darrilyn want her?'

He raked his hair. 'I don't know. No, I suppose not.'

'You could always call her bluff,' Penny told him. 'Choosing another school is hardly cause for her to change her mind.'

Matt fell into silence, feeling the weight of the world on his shoulders. How to cope with a kid he hardly knew—but a kid he loved.

The silence stretched on. Penny watched Lily. The girl was carefully piping, laughing shyly at something Noreen said. She was gangly, awkward, tentative. Even her smile was scared.

She looked like Matt.

She knew how Lily felt. She'd been given everything money could buy but no foundations.

'You can't keep her on the farm with you?'

'She's great there,' Matt told her. 'She was only

there for a week, but already she loves the animals and I think she feels safe.' He hesitated. 'Penny, I'm sorry, but it was the right call…that you left. Thank you,' he said simply and her heart gave that twist again. The twist that was all about Matt.

He'd come last night because she needed him.

'Moving on,' she managed hurriedly, because emotions were threatening to derail her. 'There's no school she can attend as a day kid?'

'Are you kidding? You know how isolated Jindalee is. I'd need to move back to the city.'

'Yeah, and you'd hate that. Making one person happy at the expense of another sucks.' She stared into the dregs of her mug and then looked again at the two girls, who were now giggling over designs for clothes for their homeless gingerbread. Lily… Matt's daughter…

And suddenly—where it came from she could never afterwards figure—she had such a surge of bonding that she couldn't explain.

Maybe she could help.

'Adelaide's a lot closer to Jindalee than Sydney,' she said slowly. 'And Noreen's from Adelaide. She came to Sydney following a boy. It didn't work out.'

'Yeah?' He obviously wasn't following.

'There's nothing holding me here either,' she said.

He'd been watching the girls. Now he turned and stared. 'Penny, what are you suggesting?'

'I know a good boarding school in Adelaide. One of the Aussie girls at finishing school in Switzerland told me about it. They run a decent academic programme but they also have their own farm. There's an emphasis on things other than academia. Lots of camping, hands-on stuff, fun. Alice told me it was the only time in her life she'd felt she belonged.'

'I need the details.'

'Yeah, but it won't be enough,' she told him. 'Lily needs a base in Adelaide. She'll know no one outside school.'

'I can get an apartment and be there whenever I'm needed. Or I'll stay if I must.'

'And leave the farm completely? That'd suck.'

'I'll do it if I need to.'

Of course he would, because this was Matt.

But maybe… Maybe she could help. *I am woman.*

Matt was a friend. Women helped their friends. And didn't this fit into her plans anyway?

'It's early days yet, but if she likes the school… Matt, if you think it might work, maybe I could set myself up in Adelaide?' And then, as his face creased into a frown, she rushed on.

'I've decided not to stay in Sydney,' she told him. 'This place is temporary while I sort things out, apply for finance, put a business plan together. My hope is to set up a catering company in a city other than this one. Noreen would love to go home to Adelaide with her pride intact and I'm thinking we could search for premises near Lily's school. It would mean she doesn't feel so alone. With your permission, she could drop in after classes. She'd have you coming back and forth, and my place as a backup when you're not there.'

'Why would you do that?' he asked at last. 'Penny, what are you offering?'

'Not much,' she said diffidently. 'Lily might not need or want me but it doesn't matter. And it might end up working for us both.'

'To move your whole life…'

'Hey, it's better than cooking at Malley's,' she said and grinned. 'And I need to move somewhere.' She took a deep breath. 'Where Mum got the courage from I don't know, but we've talked and she's decided to leave Dad. She should have done it years ago. Dad's had mistress after mistress but she's tried to keep everyone happy. It'll take decent lawyers to extricate her money from Dad's clutches, but now… You saw the way she pulled you into dinner last night. She's a born hostess. I see her as the front man for my company.'

'But… Adelaide? For Lily?'

She hesitated, still watching Lily. It was a good way not to look at Matt.

'Matt, this isn't a sacrifice,' she told him. 'Who knows if Lily will even need somewhere like my kitchen after she's settled? Who knows whether my mum will like Adelaide, and who knows if Adelaide likes my kind of catering?'

'But you'll do it for Lily.'

'Lily could be a deciding factor,' she confessed. 'But it's no big deal. Helping your daughter seems right. We are friends, are we not?'

'No,' he said forcibly, and he said it so loudly that Lily and Noreen stopped what they were doing and turned and stared.

'No, Penny, we're not friends. Or not *just* friends. Penny Hindmarsh-Firth, I said it before and I hardly believed that I'd said it. But I believe it now. I believe that I love you.'

In a romance movie she might have fallen into his arms right then. Hero declares his love. Heroine swoons with joy.

She wasn't having a bar of it.

I am woman...

In an hour a van would arrive from the homeless refuge and she'd promised a meal for fifty. She didn't have time to sit around and listen to declarations of love.

Because she had qualms and she wasn't falling for a line she'd heard before.

She'd been nice to his daughter and he'd told her he loved her. But she had no intention of being loved because she was needed. Of being loved because she'd done the right thing.

Not any more.

There was a part of her that would have allowed Matt to sweep her up in his arms and carry her off into the sunset with violins playing in the background.

She wanted him—but not on those terms.

So… *Get thee back*, she told the insidious voice in her head that would have welcomed being carried off on whatever terms Matt offered. But she'd been burned too often. She'd spent her life trying to please her father, learning from her mother that love meant sacrifice. Heaven, she'd almost married the despicable Brett because of it.

And then she'd fallen heart over head in love with Matt and broken her heart when she'd had to leave. And yes, leaving had made sense on all sorts of levels, but Matt had let her go. Two weeks ago she'd stood on his veranda and part of her had felt like dying.

She'd been burned too often. How could she believe?

'Why don't you kiss him?' Noreen asked. Both girls were watching, fascinated, but Penny turned away from Matt with a disbelieving snort and headed back to her pies.

'Because it's cupboard love,' she said, fighting to keep her voice light. To keep the whole thing light.

'It's like giving a kid a cookie. Will you love me if I give you this cookie?'

'Hey, Dad.' Lily picked up one of her luridly dressed gingerbread ladies. 'Will you love me if I give you this cookie?'

And Matt looked at Penny for a long, long moment while emotion went zinging back and forth between them. But finally he nodded gravely, as if acceding to an unspoken request.

He turned to his daughter.

'I surely will,' he said and headed over to eat the proffered cookie.

Good. That was the way she wanted it—wasn't it?

How else can I have it? she thought. *How can I trust?*

And then she thought, maybe it had just been a throwaway line after all.

Penny... I love you.

Easily said.

Prove it, she whispered under her breath. But why should he prove it?

'Am I still invited to your sister's wedding?' he asked and she blinked. Felicity's wedding. Okay, life had to go on.

'My mother invited you.' She was fiddling with the oven. She didn't turn round to face him. She daren't.

'So that's a yes?'

'If it's still on. I told Felicity…'

'She won't cancel a wedding,' Matt told her. 'Besides, they suit. Will you be leaving from your parents' house?'

'I…yes. Mum and I have decided to stay until after the wedding. We don't dislike Felicity enough to cause a media furore beforehand.'

'So what time would you like me to meet you?'

She turned to face him. 'Matt…'

'Penny.' He smiled that gorgeous, heart-warming smile that had her totally befuddled. 'I still want to come. Your mum says you need me.'

'I don't want to need you.'

His smile faded. 'Really?'

'Really.'

'Even if it's a two-way deal?'

'I don't know what you're talking about,' she said shortly, breathlessly. And then, more seriously, 'Matt, I need time. I know you can hurt me and I don't like that I'm exposed. I'm trying to get myself back together. To find who I really am. Falling for you complicates things.'

'It might simplify things.'

Noreen and Lily were watching with fascination but it couldn't matter. What needed to be said was too important.

'How?' she demanded. 'Matt, I've just come from a very messy relationship. I've spent my life watching my mother ruin her life trying to please everyone. I won't do the same.'

'If I swore to spend my life making you happy…'

'Matt, don't,' she said breathlessly. The memory of that moment on the veranda was still so raw it made her cringe. It made her block her heart from what was happening. 'I can't,' she said. 'It's too soon. I can't get my head around it. I can't…'

'Trust?'

'Exactly.' She shook her head. 'I'm sorry.'

'No, I'm sorry,' he said gently. 'Maybe if I hadn't met your family I wouldn't have understood, but I do. Penny, let's give this time.'

'I won't…'

'You might,' he told her and he came back to take her hands. He tugged her forward and kissed her. It was a light kiss, a fleeting touch of lips, but it was enough for her to know she was in serious trouble. But then he put her away and the smile he gave her was rueful.

'Saturday,' he told her. 'Wedding. What time?'

'Four. But…'

'I'll pick you up,' he told her. 'If I see you sweep out in one of the bridal limousines I'll know you don't want me to come but if you decide you want me then I'll be there. But no pressure, Penny, love. Lily and I will fly to Adelaide and check out this new school but we won't make any decisions and

you shouldn't either. We'll see you Saturday—
or not.'

'Matt…'

'No decisions,' he said again and he turned to
Lily. 'Ready to go?' he asked her. 'Penny's suggested a new school you might like. Are you ready
to try again?'

'I don't know whether I'm brave enough,' Lily
whispered.

'That makes all of us,' Matt told her. 'Where can
we buy courage?'

CHAPTER TWELVE

IT'S A HAPPY bride the sun shines on...

Felicity should be gloriously happy, Penny decided, as she fiddled with a recalcitrant wrap and gave her reflection one last glance before heading downstairs. The sun had been shining all day.

She doubted Felicity had noticed. Felicity's six perfectly matched and beautiful bridesmaids had filled the house since morning and the place had been chaotic.

Penny had snuck out at dawn and taken a long walk around the harbour front. She'd come back an hour before they had to leave.

Even that was too early. She'd taken half an hour to dress and now she was pacing.

Matt had said he'd come, but why would he? He'd gone to Adelaide with Lily. Why would he come all the way back?

There was a faint tap on her door. Her mother was there, looking magnificent. And anxious.

'Is he coming?'

'I don't know,' Penny said shortly. She glanced at her watch. 'But we should go. It'd be nice to sneak into place before the media gets its hype together.'

'There won't be hype over me. I'm not exactly mother of the bride,' Louise told her. Felicity's mother would be sitting in the front pew with George. Penny suspected she and her mother would be relegated to a pew quite a way back.

But, even now, Louise was still trying to keep her family happy, Penny thought. She'd made the decision to leave George but she wouldn't do it until after the wedding. Instead she'd stay in the background and try and smooth things over.

'You're a very nice woman,' Penny told her and kissed her and Louise blushed and gave her a tentative hug back. But she still looked worried.

'I was sure Matt would be here.'

'It doesn't matter that he's not.'

'But Penny…'

'We can manage on our own, Mum,' she told her. 'Who needs men?'

'Yes, but Matt…'

'He's just another guy,' Penny said airily and swallowed her pride as best she could and hooked her arm into her mother's. 'Let's go slink into our back pew. You want to ride in my little pink car? Come on, Mum, let's get this thing over and done with and then we can get on with the rest of our lives.'

And she propelled her mother out of the room, down the stairs, out of the front door—where Matt was waiting.

* * *

He took her breath away.

He was standing in front of probably the world's most beautiful—and expensive—four-door sports car.

The gleaming white car looked as breathtaking as the guy leaning nonchalantly beside it. Or almost.

Because this was Matt.

He was wearing a deep black dinner suit, a suit that seemed to have been moulded onto him. It screamed Italian designer, bespoke quality. His crisp white shirt accentuated his gorgeous tanned skin, his hair seemed even darker than usual and his shoes gleamed almost as much as the car.

And his face… It was strong, angular and weathered. His crinkly eyes were smiling straight at her.

'Good afternoon,' he said formally to both of them but oh, his eyes were only for her. 'You're a little earlier than we expected but we came prepared.'

She managed to tear her eyes from Matt and saw Lily in the back seat. The window was down. 'H… hi,' Lily managed and emerged to join her father. Matt took her hand and led her forward.

The girl was wearing a pale blue frock, deceptively simple. Strappy white sandals. A single pearl necklet and earrings.

She looked very young and very lovely and also very nervous.

'Louise, this is my daughter, Lily,' Matt told her

and there was no disguising his pride. 'Lily, this is Mrs Hindmarsh-Firth.'

'Lily, call me Louise. Oh, my dear, you look perfectly beautiful. And how brave of you to let your father drag you to a wedding where you know no one.' And Lily was embraced in a cloud of expensive perfume.

Matt gave Penny a grin and a thumbs up that said a grandma-type figure was what he'd hoped for. And Penny thought this was just what her mother needed, too. Someone to mother. And then she thought—they'd arrive at the wedding *en famille*.

This was a day she'd been dreading, and her mother must have been dreading it just as much.

Louise would have walked up the aisle as a second wife, the odd one out. Penny would have walked up the aisle as a jilted bride. Now, they'd arrive at the church in this car. With this man. Together.

'Ready to go?' he asked and she managed to smile back.

'Oh, Matt…'

'Don't say a word,' he told her and he kissed his fingers and then put them gently on her lips. 'Let's just soak up our first family wedding.'

And that was breathtaking all over again.

Penny had expected to walk down the aisle as the ugly duckling. The sister who'd been dumped for the more beautiful model. She'd thought people would be looking at her with sympathy.

But as she walked down the aisle with Matt beside her she felt as if she were floating, and who cared who was looking at her?

She almost felt like a bride herself.

Louise was right behind them, holding Lily's hand. Somehow it had seemed natural to do it this way. Matt and Penny. Louise and Lily.

They slid into the pew reserved for Stepmother. As Penny had predicted, it was well back. Felicity's mother had decreed the seating arrangements for the bride's side and it was a slap to Louise. Louise was used to such slaps, as was Penny, but now it didn't affect them.

It made it harder for all the necks craning to see who they were, but Penny didn't care about that either.

Penny and Matt and Lily and Louise.

Mum and Dad and Daughter and Grandma?

She peeked a look at Louise and her mother was beaming. *Oh, Matt...* Of all the ways to dispel sympathy. They'd have the church agog as to this new order.

Had Matt known?

She dared to look up at him and found him smiling.

'You knew,' she breathed. 'The car.' She looked at him again. 'The suit.'

'I figured it might help,' he admitted. 'A bit of bling.'

'I can't begin to tell you…'

'Then don't,' he told her and grinned and held her hand tighter.

And turned to watch the wedding.

It was the perfect wedding. It was orchestrated to the last minute detail.

It was faintly…boring?

'I'm sure we can think of a better way to do this,' Matt whispered as the groom kissed the bride and six perfect bridesmaids and six beautiful grooms-men lined up to march out of the church—and Penny almost stopped breathing.

'Matt…'

'I know. It's far too soon,' he told her cheerfully and went back to watching the truly impressive bridal procession. And Penny tried really hard to start breathing again.

And then they were outside, still in a tight family group. Louise was clutching Lily's hand as if she were in danger of drowning, and Penny thought how inspired had Matt been to organise it this way.

For Lily was intelligent enough to know she was needed. The memories of her week at her horrid school had obviously been put aside. She looked lovely and she knew it. She was even beaming at the cameras.

And there were plenty of cameras. Media attention should have been on the bride and groom but it wasn't.

For, as the crowd clustered round in the sunshine, someone twigged.

'Isn't that…? Surely it's not… No, I'm certain…'

It started as a ripple, a rumour, but in seconds it was a wave of certainty.

'Matthew Fraser! Owner of Harriday Holdings!'

'Surely not!'

'I'm sure. My dear, he's possibly the richest man in the country. But he's intensely private. Oh, my heaven… Didn't they say it was Brett who dumped Penelope? Goodness, maybe it was the other way around.'

Penny could see the wave of amazement, the wash of speculation—and the absolute switch of attention.

The media was suddenly all over them.

But it still didn't matter. Matt's hold on her hand tightened. He kept Louise and Lily in his circle.

The feeling of family deepened.

She'd dreaded this wedding but the dread had gone.

This wedding felt like her own.

The reception was on the Harbour, in a restaurant with a view to die for. But of course they were seated right at the back, on a table with others

Felicity's mother had deemed insignificant. They were placed with the vicar who'd conducted the marriage service and his lively wife and three great-aunts.

For someone who lived alone, Matt did an extraordinary job of pulling people together, and Louise helped. She hadn't been meant to sit with them—that would have been too big an insult to seat her so far back—but she insisted on staying. She and Matt were determined to make their table lively. The great-aunts rose to the occasion. The vicar's wife announced that she'd attended Lily's new school in Adelaide and proceeded to tell scandalous stories of the teachers.

Lily visibly relaxed and so did Penny. She sat back and watched Matt weave his magic, and the feelings she had for him grew stronger and stronger.

Who was he doing this for? His daughter? He'd turned her into a princess for the night.

Penny's mother? Louise was charmed and charming. This day had turned out to be so different to the one she'd dreaded.

The great-aunts? These were three spinsters, insignificant aunts of Louise, but Penny and Louise both loved them. And they loved Matt.

They were having fun.

They had people at the other tables staring, and

Penny was starting to see an almost universal wish. Theirs was suddenly the party table.

The dancing started. Bride and groom. Then the groom's parents—and Felicity's mother with George.

This was the moment when it would have truly sucked to be Louise, but suddenly Matt was on his feet, propelling Louise to the dance floor to be the fourth couple, and if Penny hadn't been in love with him already she fell right then.

Her mother wasn't the insignificant other. Matt was heart-meltingly handsome, and he swirled her mother round the dance floor as if she were a queen.

As other couples poured onto the floor she tugged Lily up and they had fun. The vicar and his wife came out to join them and then they swept down on the great-aunts.

'We can't dance if we don't have partners,' the great-aunts said in horror, but Lily put them straight.

'That's so last century,' Matt's daughter pronounced. 'Waiting for a guy to ask you is sexist and dumb. Get with it.'

So then they were all on the floor, and the great-aunts were teaching Lily to jive and Matt and Louise joined them—and then somehow Matt had hold of Penny, steering her effortlessly away from the giggling jivers—and somehow everything around them seemed to slide into oblivion.

* * *

The music changed to a rhumba and Matt was good. Very good. Penny could dance a mean rhumba herself and it felt as if she was almost part of him.

His hand held hers, tight, strong, warm. He tugged her in and out again, swung her, danced effortlessly, held her gaze the entire time.

She felt like Cinderella at the ball, she thought wildly, and then she wondered: *Is there a midnight?*

Surely there had to be a catch.

'Where did you learn to dance?' she managed as they swung. She was breathless, laughing, stunned.

'My mum,' he said simply. 'I think she had me dancing before I could walk.'

'You do still love her then?' She said it wonderingly.

His smile faded a little but the warmth was still there. 'She was an appalling mother, but I couldn't stop loving her.' The dance had him tugging her into him, and he brushed her hair with a fleeting kiss before the moves pushed them apart again.

'It seems once I give my heart, it breaks me apart to get it back,' he said simply. 'Loving seems to be forever. Is that scary? Yes, it is. Is it contagious? I hope so.'

Out she swung and then in again, but this time his arm didn't propel her out again.

Instead he held her close, closer, and closer still. He kissed her.

* * *

It was her sister's wedding day. The focus of the entire day should be on Felicity.

Penny stood in the middle of the dance floor and melted into Matt's arms and let him kiss her.

For how could she pull away from Matt?

The kiss was plundering, deep, hot, a public declaration but a private vow. The music faded to nothing. There was only each other.

And half Australia's polite society.

She didn't care. She kissed him back, with all the love in her heart, and she thought: *If this night is all I have, then I'm Cinderella.*

And finally, when the kiss stopped, as all kisses eventually must, when she finally stood at arm's length, when he smiled down at her, just smiled and smiled, she knew where her heart was. She knew there'd be no midnight.

As the dancers around them erupted into laughing applause she blushed, but Matt held her hand and she held his hand back.

'Hey, Penelope.' It was a reporter from the biggest society tabloid in the country, calling from the side of the room as Matt led her back to the table. 'How's it feel to be the jilted bride?'

And there was only one word to say to that.

'Perfect.'

Because it was.

* * *

Lily wilted. Matt needed to take her home and the entire table decided to follow.

'I know you're supposed to wait for the bride to leave,' one great-aunt grumbled. 'But these days they stay until three in the morning and if *you* leave, young man, there's not a person in this room who can criticise us.'

'And you don't know your way around this part of town,' Louise declared. She wasn't about to let the night end on a whimper. 'Let's make the grand exit.'

So they said their goodbyes—politely, but *en masse*—and departed and Matt thought the bride and groom would be pleased to see them go. Brett had been sending him dark looks all night. Felicity had been carefully avoiding looking at her half-sister.

They'd have much more fun without them.

'But drop in tomorrow,' Penny's father said to Matt, clapping him on the shoulder. He'd learned by now who he'd patronized five days ago.

'Thank, you, sir, but I'm heading back to Adelaide tomorrow,' Matt told him. 'I have a daughter to settle into school.'

He smiled and held Lily by one hand and Penny with the other and led them out. It was a defiant little team and it felt great.

And then they were outside, breathing in the warm night air of Sydney Harbour, and he felt Penny almost slump beside him.

'Done?' he said gently. 'Not so bad at all, really.'

'Thanks to you,' she whispered. 'Matt, if you knew what you've done... For Mum... For me...'

'Sort of like charging in and cooking for a shearing team of twenty,' he told her. 'But with far less work.'

'Are you really heading back to Adelaide tomorrow?'

'Um...no,' he told her. The great-aunts and Louise were at his back and Lily was beside him. He needed to choose his words with care. 'I thought I might head back tonight, if it's okay with you.'

'Tonight?' Her face became still and he thought, he hoped, it was disappointment. But the expression was fleeting. Penny had herself under control.

She'd been verbally slapped too many times, he thought. He wouldn't mess with this woman again.

Ever.

'Of course it's okay with me,' she was saying but he shook his head.

'Don't say that until you hear my plan.'

'What plan?'

'I thought I'd take you with me.'

There was a gasp from the great-aunts and from Louise. Not from Lily, though. His daughter was grinning.

She'd been in on this plan and was loving it.

'What…why?'

'I have things I need to show you,' he told her. 'Important things. Lily and I have been busy.'

'I thought you were looking at schools.'

'We have been,' he told her. 'Lily's planning to try out the school you recommended as a day kid, before deciding to try boarding. Boarding there looks fun but we're taking this slowly. Meanwhile, we have a master plan and I want to share it with you.'

'So…you'll both fly back tonight.'

'Not Lily,' he told her. 'Lily's exhausted, aren't you, Lily?'

And Lily looked at him and grinned. She'd made an excellent show of wilting inside the wedding venue, but now she was all smiles.

'I'm so tired,' she said meekly.

'So we're taking her back to the hotel on the way to the airport,' Matt told Penny.

'You can't leave her alone!'

'Who said anything about leaving her alone? Noreen's booked in with her. It took a bit of trouble to track her down but we managed it. Staying in the Caledonian, all expenses paid—Noreen thinks it will be awesome. Tomorrow they're taking the ferry over to Manly to check out the beach. They'll have two nights together while Lily recovers from her very exhausting night tonight…'

'I'm so exhausted,' Lily added, her smile widening. She looked so like her father!

'And they'll both fly over to Adelaide on Monday,' Matt told the speechless Penny. 'How about that for a plan?'

'Hey,' Louise said. 'What about me?'

'Hey, yourself,' Matt told her and grinned. He was no longer holding Penny's hand. He'd tugged her in so she was hugged against him. 'You're included anywhere you want to be included.' But then he reconsidered. 'Though not tonight. Not with us. But the girls would love a chaperone tomorrow.'

'I could take them to my very favourite restaurant for lunch,' Louise told him and smiled at Lily. 'My friend Beth has a son who's a lifeguard at Manly. Do you think you and Noreen would like surfing lessons?'

'Wow,' Lily breathed. 'Wow!'

Louise hesitated. 'I might stay at the Caledonian too. If that's okay with you.'

'Come over to Adelaide on Monday with the girls,' Matt told her. 'I think Penny would love it.'

'Hey, what about us?' one of the great-aunts demanded. 'This sounds fun.'

'Any and all of you are welcome,' Matt said, hugging Penny tighter. 'As of Monday, but not before if you don't mind.' He glanced at his watch. 'Apologies, folk, but I have a private jet chartered in an hour. My plan includes sweeping Penny away...'

'Sweeping?' Penny gasped.

'Sweeping.' He smiled broadly. 'But not without a plan. I'm sweeping you up in my jet and taking you off to places unknown and I'm keeping you only unto me until Monday. And, before you start with the practicalities, I had a conversation with your father's esteemed butler and it turns out he's a romantic at heart. He has a bag packed and one dog, brushed and fed and ready to go. A confirmation phone call from you, and they'll be on the tarmac waiting for us.' And then he couldn't help himself. He swept her up into his arms and held her close. His dark eyes gleamed. 'If that's okay with you, darling Penny.'

She thought suddenly of her lonely drive across outback Australia in her little pink car. Woman and dog.

I am woman...

She'd thought she was strong. She'd thought she'd cope alone.

And she was, she thought mistily. Except right now she was woman in the middle of...love.

Her family. Her mum, her great-aunts. Lily.

Her man.

'*I am woman*,' she whispered to Matt as he held her close. 'I can do anything I want.'

'I'm sure you can,' he told her. 'So what do you want?'

'I want to be with you.'

CHAPTER THIRTEEN

PENTHOUSE SUITE. Adelaide's most prestigious hotel. Gorgeous, gorgeous, gorgeous.

They'd arrived at two in the morning and Penny had hardly noticed her surroundings.

She didn't notice them now. She was spooned in the great wide bed, her body moulded, skin to skin, with the man she loved with all her heart.

She had no idea where this was going. She had no idea how their lives could mesh, but for now all she cared about was that she was with Matt. And somehow things had been taken out of her hands. The great swell of loneliness she'd felt practically all her life had suddenly been lifted.

Last night had been fun, she thought dreamily. Her sister's wedding, an event she'd been dreading, had turned out to be an event where she'd felt she'd belonged for the first time in her life.

Because of the man who held her in his arms right now.

A sunbeam was playing on her face. She felt warm, loved. She had no intention of stirring, but somehow Matt must have sensed her wakefulness.

He opened his eyes, tugged her closer and she felt him smile.

She wriggled around so she faced him, looping her arms around his neck and she thought: *If I could hold this moment... This is where I want to be for the rest of my life.*

But there was a whimper from the floor beside them and the outside world broke in, in the form of one small dog.

'I need to...' she started but Matt tugged her tight with one hand and reached for the phone with the other.

'You don't need to do anything,' he told her, and a minute later a discreet hotel employee arrived. Matt donned a bathrobe, and Samson and his leash—and a discreet bank note—were handed over. Matt returned to bed, his dark eyes gleaming.

'Now, where were we?'

It took them a while to surface. Samson was obviously being taken for a very long walk.

'He's having breakfast downstairs,' Matt told her when she managed to ask. 'Speaking of breakfast, we need room service. Can I interest you in croissants? An omelette? Champagne? Okay, maybe not champagne. We have things to do, you and me.'

'Really?'

'Or things to see,' he told her. 'Though how can I look at anything else when you're right here?' He kissed her and croissants were put on the back burner for a while.

An hour later, dressed in her very favourite jeans and sweater—*how had Brian managed that?*—

they were in an open-topped roadster heading for the hills. Literally.

'It's where Lily's school is,' he told her and that was where she thought he was taking her. But instead he pulled up outside an eclectic, fashionable village-type shopping centre, lined with trees, full of enticing cafés and Sunday morning visitors.

He helped her out of the car, tucked Samson under one arm, took her hand and led her to the end of the street. Then he paused.

He stopped in front of a building that looked like an old warehouse. It was built of clinker brick, weathered with age, long and low and looking as if it was part of the land around them. It had only one storey, but the roof rose in the middle to form a rectangle of clerestory windows.

Huge barn-like doors looked as if they were built of solid oak. A smaller entrance door was built within, so one person could go in, or twenty.

It was beautiful.

There was a 'For Sale' sign out the front. A notice had been plastered over it: 'Contract Pending'.

'Want to see?' Matt asked and Penny turned her attention from the gorgeous old brick building and looked up at Matt. He looked anxious.

'Matt...'

'Nothing's final,' he said hurriedly. 'This is your decision. But come inside.'

And he opened the small door and ushered her in.

Outside it was lovely. Inside it was perfect.

It took her breath away.

It was already set up as a commercial kitchen. Great wooden benches ran along the middle of the hall. Sinks were inserted at regular intervals. More benches lined the walls with a bank of commercial ovens. There were massive dishwashers, heating banks, storage...

There was a loading ramp at the back so vans could back in. A rear door could be opened and food loaded.

'There's parking for six trucks at the rear,' Matt told her and he still sounded anxious.

'It's perfect,' Penny breathed. Samson was down on the floor, investigating smells left from a hundred years of baking. 'Wow.'

'It's an old bakery,' Matt told her. 'The original ovens are still out the back.'

'So I could make wood-fired bread. I could...'

He put a finger on her lips. 'Wait until you see the rest,' he told her. 'It's a package deal.'

And he led her out the back, across the car park and through a small garden. There were two small cottages, side by side. Built as a pigeon pair.

He opened the door of the first and she saw perfection. Two bedrooms. An open fire. Sunlight streaming through the windows.

Modern touches, subtly adding every comfort.

'It's a package deal,' Matt repeated as she prowled in wonder. 'Two cottages or nothing. Penny, it's only five minutes' walk from Lily's school.' Suddenly he sounded almost apologetic. 'I thought…I hoped…'

And then he stopped, as if what he was about to say was too big to put into words.

She turned and held his hands and smiled up at him, and she thought her heart might burst. But she waited for what he might say.

'I thought…for the first few months, until she's settled, I could stay here,' he told her. 'Well, I'll stay in Adelaide anyway. I'll pay someone to manage Jindalee but I'll go home at weekends. I can organize a chopper to go back and forth, daily if needed. If Lily's a day kid she can come back and forth at weekends too. I thought…you could have one cottage and Lily and I could have the other. Unless…'

'Unless?' She could scarcely breathe.

And then she stopped breathing entirely, because he had both her hands in his and his smile was uncertain, tremulous, but filled with such hope…

'It's too soon to ask you,' he told her. 'I know that. It's unfair to put pressure on you. But Penny, my feelings won't change. I've figured that out about myself. My heart seems to have a will of its own. I figured I'd be alone for ever but I was wrong. Penny, if you allow me to buy this…'

'I…allow…!'

'This is your place,' he told her. 'Lily and I both knew it the moment we saw it. I have no doubt you could raise the capital to buy it yourself, but it would be my very great honour to buy it for you. With no strings attached.'

'No strings?'

'Except…maybe once a month for the next six months, you allow me to ask you to marry me. No pressure to accept. Just listen to my proposal. And every month I'll think of more reasons why you should. At the end of those six months, if you're still unsure, I'll walk away. I promise. So it's a small string. One question, once a month.'

'And that's the cost of my lease?' She could scarcely make her voice work.

'Not a lease. A sale. My weekly proposal doesn't make a difference as to whether you'll own it or not.' The hold on her hands grew tighter. 'So, my love, what will it be? Do we have a deal?'

She shook her head. Somehow she made herself smile although she could feel tears welling behind her eyes.

'The cost being six proposals?'

'Yes.'

'Then how can that work?' she whispered. 'How can that possibly work when I'm answering your

proposal right now. The building is sold. Of course
I'll marry you, Matt Fraser. With all of my heart.'

It was a wedding with a difference. A Jindalee
wedding.

Matt Fraser had been a recluse for most of his
life. He wasn't a recluse any more but this was no
huge wedding. This was a wedding for the closest
of their family and friends and no one else.

The reception was to be held back at the homestead because the caterers—Penny's team, led by
the now indomitable Noreen—couldn't cart the
food all the way to the river. But the ceremony
itself was held at the billabong Matt had shown
Penny after shearing.

Expecting guests to arrive on horseback was too
big an ask, but they'd had time to build a carefully
concealed track. The wedding was twelve months
in the planning.

Which wasn't quite true, Penny thought as she
rode steadily to the place where she and Matt were
to be married. They hadn't spent twelve months
planning a wedding. They'd spent twelve months
building a life together.

For the first few months Matt had commuted
back and forth between Jindalee and Adelaide. He
now had his pilot's licence—and his own chopper.
He'd built up his flying hours fast as he flew back
and forth a couple of times a week.

He could have made his home in Adelaide but neither Penny nor Lily wanted it.

Lily boarded at her new school and loved it.

Penny had established a catering firm that was already inundated with more orders than she could handle.

And at weekends they all went home.

Home. Jindalee.

The farm looked magnificent, Penny thought, as Maisie plodded steadily on, with Ron and Harv riding side by side as her proud escorts. Matt would have bought her a younger mare, as he'd bought a lovely bay mare for Lily, but Penny and Maisie had developed a bond she had no intention of breaking. Maisie went so slowly she had time to admire the scenery, the rolling hills, the lush pasture, the contentedly grazing sheep.

This year's shearing had been the time when she'd finally handed the day-to-day running of her company over to Noreen. Shearing had been when she'd come home.

It felt good. No, it felt great.

Lily was still coming home most weekends, although Louise was now living permanently in Adelaide. The two were as close to grandmother-grandchild as made no difference. A cottage behind the old brick bakery was home for Louise and a second home for all of them.

248 STRANDED WITH THE SECRET BILLIONAIRE

'We're late already,' Ron warned her. 'You want to get that nag to hurry up?'

'Maisie doesn't do hurry,' she said contentedly and it was just as well. She'd decided to do the full bridal bit, which meant she felt like a cloud of white lace, riding side-saddle with an immaculately groomed Samson up before her. She couldn't hurry.

Nor did she want to. This was a ride to be savoured.

And suddenly Lily was thinking of a wedding twelve months ago... The wedding Felicity had stolen.

How lucky am I? she thought, wonderingly. *How blessed?*

And then they reached the ridge down to the water. The newly made track made it easy. The guests were there and waiting, on chairs set up on the mossy grasses by the waterfall.

Lily was waiting to help her down, in full bridesmaid splendour. And Louise. They fussed about her dress, clucking that it had crushed a little during the ride. Smoothing it down. Her mother was smiling through tears and Lily was handing her her bouquet.

Penny hardly noticed.

All she saw was Matt.

He too had ridden to the wedding—on Penny's instructions. 'Because it's how I first saw you,' she'd told him. 'My knight in shining armour, on a horse to match.'

'I seem to remember I was a pretty soggy knight,' he'd told her and she'd chuckled but she'd stayed firm.

So his big black horse was calmly grazing behind the makeshift altar and Matt was standing waiting. He smiled and the world stood still.

He looked stunning. 'I'm damned if I'll wear a dinner suit if I'm riding a horse,' he'd told Penny and she'd agreed—the Matt she loved wasn't a dinner suit kind of person. But he'd compromised.

He was wearing the breeches of a true horseman, buff, moulded to his legs. He wore glossy riding boots reaching to his knees, a deep black dressage jacket and a cravat, white silk, intricate, splendid. He'd do a Regency hero proud.

He'd do anyone proud, she thought mistily. He looked spectacular. Drop dead gorgeous. Toe-curlingly handsome.

Her Matt.

Music swelled in the background. She'd thought they'd have recorded music but, amazingly, Matt seemed to have organized a grand piano. *How the...?* But now wasn't the time to ask. The pianist and a cellist were playing *A Thousand Years*, a song to take her breath away. To make all eyes well.

But she was no longer hearing the music.

Matt was smiling and smiling. Their guests were on their feet, smiling almost as much as Matt.

'Are you ready, my love?' Louise asked, groping for her lace handkerchief and then giving up and sniffing.

'Of course I'm ready,' Penny told her. 'How could I not be? This is my Matt. This is the rest of my life.'

He thought of the first time he'd seen her—little, blonde, hot and cross. Bare toes covered with sand.

He'd thought she was beautiful then. How much more so now?

The dress she'd chosen—ignoring her mother's questionable advice—was perfect for her. It was mermaid style, white silk, the bodice perfectly cupping her breasts. Tiny slivers of shoulder straps made it safe for the ride. It was figure-hugging to her hips, then flared out to her feet in a gorgeous rustle of silk and taffeta.

Shoulder straps or not, how had she ridden in that?

How could he ask? There was nothing this woman couldn't do.

Her hair was caught up loosely, curls cascading from a fragile spray of jasmine and tiny white rosebuds.

How could he look at her hair?

All he saw was her smile. And her eyes. She was smiling and smiling—just for him.

And, at that moment, something in him settled. Something strong and sure.

They hadn't hurried this wedding because it hadn't seemed important but now, here, suddenly it was.

Will you take this woman...

The words had been spoken thousands, millions of times, but they'd never been spoken as they would be today.

And now she was beside him. Lily was taking her bouquet and stepping back, and Penny was smiling up at him.

'I'm sorry I'm late,' she whispered and it was all he could do to make his voice work.

'What kept you?'

'Ron found a lamb,' she told him. 'It got through the fence down the back paddock and spent the night separated from its mum. You know we had a frost? Ron brought it in just before we left, so Noreen and I had to take the meringues out of the oven and replace them with lamb. But no drama. We have mum waiting impatiently in the home paddock, baby warming up nicely and the meringues doing their final dry in the sun on the veranda.'

And she took his breath away all over again.

'Don't tell me,' he said faintly. 'You coped with a lamb in that dress.'

'I only got it a little bit smudgy,' she told him, lifting an arm so he could see a tiny smudge of mud on her waist. 'And somehow I already had a little smear of lemon icing on the hip. But it's okay. It's pretty perfect.'

And he couldn't help himself. He chuckled and then thought: *To heck with convention.* He gathered her to him and hugged her and swept her round and round until she squealed.

And then he set her on her feet again and they both stopped laughing.

Pretty perfect? She was absolutely perfect.

Life was perfect.

They turned together, hand in hand, to be made man and wife.

* * * * *

COMING NEXT MONTH FROM

HARLEQUIN®
Romance

Available May 9, 2017

#4567 CONVENIENTLY WED TO THE GREEK
by Kandy Shepherd

Greek tycoon Alex Mikhalis will do whatever it takes to get even with the blogger who nearly destroyed his reputation—only guarded Adele Hudson isn't exactly like he remembers. And when Alex discovers she's pregnant, he soon suggests a very intimate solution: becoming his convenient wife!

#4568 HIS SHY CINDERELLA
by Kate Hardy

When racing driver Brandon Stone wants to buy her company, his shy business rival Angel McKenzie has no intention of selling! But Brandon ignites feelings in Angel she never knew existed. He's the last person she should *ever* date, but her heart is telling her to break the rules...

#4569 FALLING FOR THE REBEL PRINCESS
by Ellie Darkins

For successful music executive Charlie, AKA Princess Caroline of Afland, and rock star Joe Kavanagh, one night in Vegas changes everything... Their marriage is a PR dream come true for Joe, but as their initial attraction turns into something much deeper, can he convince Charlie that they were made for one other?

#4570 CLAIMED BY THE WEALTHY MAGNATE
The Derwent Family
by Nina Milne

One evening with wealthy lawyer Daniel Harrington makes Lady Kaitlin Derwent crave freedom from her tragic past... Daniel's never believed in love, but Kaitlin opens up new possibilities. Soon he's determined to show her that by being true to yourself you can find happiness—even in the most unexpected of places!

YOU CAN FIND MORE INFORMATION ON UPCOMING HARLEQUIN® TITLES, FREE EXCERPTS AND MORE AT WWW.HARLEQUIN.COM.

HRLPCNM0417

SPECIAL EXCERPT FROM

HARLEQUIN®

Romance

CONVENIENTLY WED TO THE GREEK
by *Kandy Shepherd*

*When Greek tycoon Alex Mikhalis discovers
Adele Hudson is pregnant, he abandons his plans
to get even and suggests a very intimate solution:
becoming his convenient wife!*

Read on for a sneak preview:

"What?" The word exploded from her. "You can't possibly be serious."

Alex looked down into her face. Even in the slanted light from the taverna she could see the intensity in his black eyes. "I'm very serious. I think we should get married."

Dell had never known what it felt to have her head spin. She felt it now. Alex had to take hold of her elbow to steady her. "I can't believe I'm hearing this," she said. "You said you'd never get married. I'm not pregnant to you. In fact you see my pregnancy as a barrier to kissing me, let alone marrying me. Have you been drinking too much ouzo?"

"Not a drop," he said. "It's my father's dying wish that I get married. He's been a good father. I haven't been a good son. Fulfilling that wish is important to me. If I have to get married, it makes sense that I marry you."

"It doesn't make a scrap of sense to me," she said. "You don't get married to someone to please someone else, even if it is your father."

Alex frowned. "You've misunderstood me. I'm not talking about a real marriage."

This was getting more and more surreal. "Not a real marriage? You mean a marriage of convenience?"

"Yes. Like people do to be able to get residence in a country. In this case it would be marriage to make my father happy. He wants the peace of mind of seeing me settled."

"You feel you owe your father?"

"I owe him so much it could never be calculated or repaid. This isn't about owing my father, it's about loving him. I love my father, Dell."

But you'll never love me, she cried in her heart. How could he talk about marrying someone—anyone—without a word about love?

Make sure to read...
CONVENIENTLY WED TO THE GREEK
by Kandy Shepherd.
Available May 2017 wherever
Harlequin® Romance books and ebooks are sold.

www.Harlequin.com

Copyright © 2017 by Kandy Shepherd

HREXP74429

HARLEQUIN® *Romance*

Next month, Harlequin® Romance author

Kate Hardy

brings you:

His Shy Cinderella

The real woman behind his rival…

Racing driver Brandon Stone is intent on proving
that he has what it takes to run his family business—
first stop: procuring rival race car designers the
McKenzies. But shy Angel McKenzie has no
intention of selling up!

Angel has avoided the limelight for most of her life.
But with her family business under threat she'll do
anything it takes to save it. Working closely with
Brandon ignites feelings she never knew existed…
he might be the last person she should *ever* date,
but her heart is telling her to break the rules!

**On sale May 2017,
only in Harlequin® Romance
Don't miss it!**

*Available wherever Harlequin® Romance books
and ebooks are sold.*

www.Harlequin.com

HR74433